Fernhill Lane

A Huckleberry Bay Novel

Kristen Proby

&
AMPERSAND
PUBLISHING, INC.

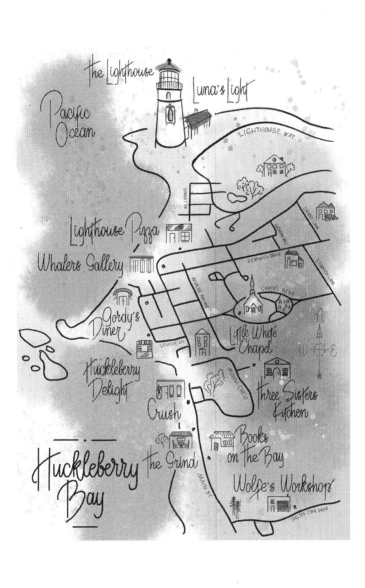

Fernhill Lane
A Huckleberry Bay Novel
By
Kristen Proby

FERNHILL LANE

A Huckleberry Bay Novel

Copyright © 2022 by Kristen Proby

Cover Design: By Hang Le

Cover photo: Wander Aguiar

This is for the girls on my proof team.
Jaime, Renee, Yvonne, Katrina, and Crystal.
You are the most supportive, amazing, badass women, and
I'm so grateful to you, not just for your hard work, but for
all of the happiness you bring to my life.
Thank you for being you.
I love you.

Prologue

Sarah

January 1, 2000

I hope my parents don't find this journal. Mama
would probably tell me that it's a waste of time, and I
should concentrate on other things, but I think it's fun,
and it's the only thing that I have for myself.

June, Luna, and I were up in the lighthouse, in our
special place, the other day, and we found a super old
diary from the 1800s. We started to read it but then
decided to only read one entry at a time so that it lasts
longer.

We also agreed to start our own diaries. So, here I am.
What do people talk about in these things? I don't want to

say anything too personal. What if Mama does find it? I'd be in deep trouble.

Not that I won't be, anyway. She'll come up with a reason to be mad at me. That's just how life is here.

I wish I could go live with Luna or June.

Anyway, the Christmas break is almost over, and it will be time to go back to school. I don't mind it so much. I'll get to see Tanner every day! I know he's a whole year older than me, but he's so handsome. And he's really nice to me. Sometimes, he walks me home from school. Isn't that the sweetest thing ever? I hope he had a nice Christmas.

I can hear Scott arguing with Dad again, so I'd better go see what's up before it gets too bad. I love my little brother, and I hate that Dad can be too hard on him. He's just a kid!

I hope I can write in this diary often. It feels kind of good to write down what I'm thinking.

TTYL,

Sarah

Chapter One

Sarah

"I forgot how busy it is in the spring," I say to my coworker, Sunny, as I grab a wet towel to wipe off a table. "We always think of summer as being the busy season, but it's really all the time."

"These days it is." She taps on the computer screen, sending an order back to the kitchen. "And I'm grateful because that means we don't have to lay anyone off during the slow season anymore."

"There is that." I shoot her a smile and hurry over to clean the table and then pass by another table to take an order.

I've been back in Huckleberry Bay for just over six months, and every single minute of every day has been a blessing.

I'm out of an abusive marriage.

I'm back in my hometown.

Life is finally the way I've daydreamed it would be for more than a decade.

"Hey, Sarah."

I've had two best friends since I was a child, and one of them just walked through the door.

"Hi, June. What can I getcha?"

"The usual," she says with a sigh. "Hey, when you get home later, can you help me tear apart Grandma's bathroom? She says there's a leak, and I can't find it. I need someone who *doesn't* have arthritis in her back to hold the flashlight for me."

"Sure." I give her a smile and then cross to the computer to tap in June's order of a cheeseburger and onion rings.

I've lived with June and her grandma in the big Victorian house on the cliffs outside of town since my apartment burned down, along with my friend Wolfe's auto mechanic garage, late last fall. And I'm grateful to June and Annabelle for giving me a place to live.

I really am.

But I do *not* want to help tear apart anything when I'm off shift. I want to go home—somewhere *quiet*—elevate my swollen feet, and curl up with a glass of wine and my cat.

Still, I'll do what she asks because I live in the house rent-free, and it's the least I can do.

The thing is, my friends, June and Luna, along with the whole town really, have been nothing but welcoming and supportive since I arrived last fall, and I'll do whatever it takes to show my gratitude.

Even if it means giving up my solitude for a little while.

"Hey, did you hear that we were able to finally get the insulation and drywall up in Luna's inn?" June asks as I slide her basket of food over to her. "It actually looks like a dwelling now."

"Luna mentioned it." I grin and wipe my hands on my apron. "I've been working on renderings for the website, and I think I'm going to go over there one evening when you're all finished so I can soak in the atmosphere. I need to get started on the paintings for the guest suites."

"It's so awesome that you're doing the artwork," June says around an onion ring. "It's going to be *killer*."

"Luna's come up with some fun themes for the suites, and I can't wait to get started. I'm sorry, I might be working late. We had another girl call out."

"It's okay," she says and bites into her burger. "I can swing back by later and pick you up."

June's been nice enough to drive me to and from work for each of my shifts. Annabelle's house is a couple of miles outside of town, and although I *could* walk, it's been nice that I don't have to.

I'm on my feet all day as it is.

"Honey, you need to go home," Sunny says as I put in another order. "This is your third double shift in a row. I've got this covered until Willow gets here."

"I don't like leaving you alone when we're busy," I reply. "Yeah, we're a diner, and these people are supposed to clean up after themselves, but most don't. And we're short-staffed. Not to mention, I can use the money."

"It's only one hour until Willow gets here. I've been working this job for more than twenty years, so trust me when I say, I've got this. Go rest up."

I sigh, feeling the exhaustion in my bones. It really has been a long, busy week.

"Are you sure you don't mind?"

"Go. And take tomorrow off, too. We'll have plenty of help."

"A day off?" I blink at her. "What shall I do with all that free time?"

"Smartass." She laughs and shakes her head. "I sure do like you."

I hurry back to the break room to grab my purse from my locker and then rush back out to June with visions of an early night dancing in my head.

There should be time for bathroom fixing *and* wine with my cat, Petunia.

"Let's blow this joint," I announce to June, who's in the middle of a conversation with Tanner Hilleman.

My high school sweetheart.

The man that still haunts my dreams.

He looks my way, his green eyes dancing as he takes me in, and a slow smile spreads over his impossibly gorgeous mouth.

And I remember vividly what the man is capable of doing with that mouth.

Clearing my throat, I offer him a smile, then tap June's shoulder.

"Ready?" I ask her. "I've been sprung a little early."

"Sure, but first, I'd like to chat for a few minutes with

Tanner. He's telling me about how his aunt down in Newport is having her kitchen redone, and it's been a total disaster."

My heart sinks, but I do my best to keep my smile in place. I just *really* want to go home. And while Tanner and I have an amicable relationship, it's still uncomfortable to be around him for very long.

It's just damn awkward.

But June is my ride, so I sit next to her and quietly listen to the story of Tanner's aunt. I liked Aunt Becky a lot when we were dating. She was always very kind to me.

I check my watch and sigh, and June's gaze turns my way.

"You okay, Sarah?"

"Sure."

"I think she's tired," Tanner replies and stands. "I've kept you long enough. I'll be sure to keep you posted on all of Aunt Becky's kitchen mishaps. Have a good evening, ladies."

He nods and leaves, and I immediately stand.

"You know, I could go for a milkshake to go," June says. "I mean, sure, I shouldn't because that's a lot of calories, but I've been busting my ass lately."

"June, I'm going to say this in the nicest way possible. Please, for the love of all that's holy in this universe, take me the hell home."

"Oh, sure. Hey, I'm sorry. Let's go."

We walk out to June's truck, and I sigh in relief when I sit in the seat.

"You've had a long week, haven't you?" June asks.

"Yeah, a lot of hours at the diner. But, I'm grateful for the job, so I won't complain. Sunny just gave me tomorrow off."

"Awesome. You should—"

"Nope."

She glances my way as she turns to drive up the hill to her grandmother's house. "Huh?"

"I shouldn't do *anything* except sleep late, go walk the beach, snuggle Petunia, and write in my journal. Maybe paint a little."

"So, I shouldn't ask you to help me with garden prep, then?"

I wince and look out the passenger window. "Please don't."

"You deserve a day of rest and pampering," June says, patting my leg. "I totally get it. I'm just too antsy for those days, so it never occurs to me, you know?"

"I know. I really need a quiet day."

"Then a quiet day you shall have."

She parks in her spot near the house, and my feet ache as I slide out of the truck onto the gravel below.

You would think that after six months or so of constantly being on my feet, they'd be used to it by now, but they're not.

"I need to soak my feet," I mutter and hobble my way up the steps to the front door.

"You need better shoes, too," June says as she opens the door, and we walk inside.

She's not wrong, I likely *do* need better footwear, but

I've been hoarding my money away so I can rent a place to live.

Shoes don't fit into that budget.

"I'm going to go see Petunia," I tell June and set off up the stairs. "I'll come help you in a bit."

"Thanks," June says. I hear her walk into the heart of the house, likely looking for Annabelle.

When I open the door of my bedroom, Petunia stretches lazily on my bed, blinks her bicolored eyes, and, with great effort, lifts herself up to come over and get some attention.

"Hi, beautiful girl," I whisper and pick her up into my arms. Petunia is a big tabby cat that I rescued shortly after I moved to town. She looked a little worse for wear at the time, but she's doing better now.

Of course, no TLC in the world will repair the ear that she lost somewhere along the way, but she's happy and spoiled, and we love each other.

I've just sat down with Petunia in my lap, when I hear the yelling start.

I love June and Annabelle with everything in me. Annabelle is the grandma I always wanted, and June is like a sister to me.

But, oh God, I can't live here anymore. I'm tired, I'm frazzled, and I'm too old for roommates.

It's time I found my own space.

"Sarah, can you come look at this please? This old lady has lost her mind."

"Lost my mind, have I? Well then, why don't I just call the lawyer and have my will changed."

"Yeah, yeah, you're just full of it."

I stare down at Petunia and sigh. "Let's look through the for rent ads, shall we?"

"This just became available a couple of days ago," Grace, the nice woman from the rental agency, says as we step out of her car. She was kind enough to pick me up for this little excursion. "It's a honey of a place, and as of right now, it's still vacant. Come on."

I'm doing my best not to get my hopes up. This place is *perfect*. I can feel it, and I haven't even gone inside yet.

The main house sits near the ocean, with a long staircase down to the sand. I've walked past this house hundreds of times over the years.

Walking the beach is my favorite thing in the world.

I didn't know, however, that the small building just behind the main house was part of the same property and was also a guesthouse.

"The owner has had this place for a couple of years now," Grace says as she unlocks the front door, "and he's always rented out this space. It's a small, one-bedroom guesthouse with a nice bathroom and an extra space that you could use for an office. It has a full kitchen, as well, and a little back patio where you could sit out with your coffee in the morning and look at the mountains. Unfortunately, there's no front porch to look out at the ocean that's only a couple of steps off the front door."

"There's an *ocean view*?" My heart leaps when I

walk past Grace into the living space and stand at the windows, staring at the little peek of ocean through the trees.

"It's not a great view because it's obstructed by the trees, but yes. You can see it."

"Ocean view," I whisper and feel like wrapping my arms around myself in a big hug. "Will he let me have my cat?"

"That might be the stinger," she says with uncertainty. "I'll have to run it by him. He usually doesn't accept pets, but he might make an exception for you."

"If he will let me have Petunia, I'll take it."

I turn back and am startled to find Tanner standing in the doorway.

"Sorry to interrupt," he says with a half smile. "I *thought* that was you, Sarah."

"Tanner, this is Sarah Pederson, and she's interested in the rental," Grace says with a smile.

"I know Sarah," he says with a nod, never taking his eyes away from me. "Would you please give us a moment, Grace?"

"Oh. Well, I suppose so." Grace clears her throat and slips out the front door, past Tanner. "Just call for me when you're done."

"I didn't realize this was your place," I say when she's out of earshot. "If I'd known—"

"You wouldn't be here?" He tips his head to the side. "Why?"

I shrug, shaking my head. "You know why. It's just awkward, that's all."

"Do you like it?"

I love it.

"It's a nice place. Does it come furnished?"

"It does, but if you didn't like something, I can take it out."

I bite my lip. Why does he have to own the most perfect rental for me in town? I *need* a furnished place because I lost everything in the fire. And it has an ocean view.

"If I'd known you wanted to move out of June's place, I would have just offered it to you," he says. "Hell, you can have it, Sarah."

"No." I shake my head and look at him squarely now. "Absolutely not. If you'll rent it to me, I'll *pay* for it. I can afford it. But I can't come without Petunia."

"The cat?"

I nod solemnly. "I'm all she has, and I won't desert her."

"I'm fine with the cat."

Hope spreads through me. "Would it be okay if I used your beach access to walk down to the sand sometimes?"

"Whenever you'd like."

I can walk to work from here, I have beach access, and the adorable little house is furnished.

But will I have to see Tanner all the time? And if I do, will it continue to be uncomfortable?

"What's your hesitation?"

He always could read me.

"I don't want to make things weird or hard. If I live

here, and if we run into each other all the time, I don't want to make it uncomfortable for you."

He lifts an eyebrow.

"Or for me."

"It's never my intention to make you uncomfortable. If it makes you feel any better, I can tell you that I rarely ever run into my tenants. I go to work early each morning, and I pretty much keep to myself, but I'm nearby if you need anything. Sarah, we see each other as often as we do because we share the same friends. Huckleberry Bay is a small town, and I refuse to give up my friends, or turn the other way whenever I see you. There are no hard feelings here."

I nod and lick my lips, then look around the space once more.

I want it. I knew it when I saw the listing online last night.

This is where I'm supposed to be.

"I'd love to live here."

He shoves his hands in his pockets and smiles, nodding. "Good. You can move in right away. Do you need help with your things?"

"No, I don't have much. Mostly just some clothes and the cat. I lost everything else in the fire."

"Wolfe's rebuilding."

"I know. But it'll take a while. And as much as I love June, and I'm so incredibly grateful to her and Annabelle, I really need my own place, you know?"

"I get it." He pulls his hand out of his pocket and holds up a key. "Looks like this is yours, then. The rent covers all the utilities, and it's due by the fifth of the month."

"I can do that." I reach out and take the key, brushing his fingers with mine in the process.

His hand returns to his pocket.

"I can bring the money for first and last month's rent and the deposit later today."

"Whenever," he says with a shrug. "I'm in no hurry, and I know where you live. Welcome home, Sarah."

He winks, and then he walks out. Several seconds later, Grace returns with a happy smile. "I'm so glad this worked out for you! I think you'll love it here. Now, if you don't mind, I'll have to take you back to Annabelle's because I have another showing in just a bit."

"Of course." I turn back to take it all in. The small but efficient kitchen, the living space with a loveseat, chair, and TV, and that incredible view of the water.

I'm going to move in today.

"You're doing WHAT?" June demands with her hands on her hips. I had Grace drop me off at the lighthouse where June's working on the inn, and to my delight, Luna was with June, so I could tell the story once.

"She's moving into her own place," Luna says and pulls me in for a hug. "I'm so happy for you."

"Thank you."

"You don't have to move," June insists.

"Honey, I *do* have to move." I wince but stand firm. "I

love you and your grandmother, more than you'll ever know, and I'm so grateful that you let me stay with you when I didn't have anywhere else to go. But it's tough living outside of town without a vehicle, and I just want my own quiet space."

"I get it," June says with a sigh. "I just love having you there because you were gone for so long, you know?"

"I'm only moving into town, not to another country." I wrap my arms around her and hug her close. "Thank you for loving me so much, and for taking such good care of me. But, I've got this, Juniper Rose. I promise."

"Now I'm getting sloppy." June brushes at a tear on her cheek. "Okay, you're evicted. Go move in with Tanner and fall in love again."

"Whoa. That's not at *all* what's going to happen."

"I mean, it *could* happen," Luna points out, but I shake my head emphatically.

"No. That ship sailed long ago, and now he's a friend, as well as my landlord. That's it. Just wait until you see it, you guys."

"When are you moving in?" Luna asks.

"Today."

June blows out a breath. "Come on. Let's go get your stuff and your mangy cat, then get you moved."

"I'm coming, too. I can't wait to see it," Luna says.

"I love you guys. And Petunia is *not* mangy. Anymore."

June 8, 2003

Dear Diary,

I got a job! I start at Gordy's on Friday. Now that school's out for the summer, and I'm sixteen, I can have a summer job. I'm so excited. Having my own money will be so nice. I can take care of myself and Scott, and we won't have to depend on Mom and Dad so much. They don't do much for us anyway, and I'm sick of having to mooch off our friends for food.

I know they say that it's not a big deal, but it's still embarrassing. I'll buy groceries for Scott and me, and I'll hide them.

I don't get to wait tables yet because I don't have enough experience, but it'll be okay to clear them and help wherever they need me. Gordy said that some of the servers will share some of their tips with me, and that would be cool.

Tanner Hilleman asked me out on a date, so basically, this is the best week that's ever happened. We're going to the movies Friday night. I don't know what to wear, so I'll have to ask the girls to help me.

A job, a cute boy, and SUMMER. *Yeehaw!*
TTYL,
Sarah

Chapter Two

Tanner

"Right?"

I blink and try to focus on the young woman speaking to me about a seascape painting hanging on the wall of my gallery. She's been droning on and on, and I drowned her out with thoughts of Sarah.

"I'm sorry, would you mind repeating that?"

"I was just saying, the colors in this are so vibrant. It looks like there's about to be a thunderstorm over the water here, and it makes me want to curl up with a blanket and a book." She laughs and tosses her dark hair over one shoulder. "Which means I probably *shouldn't* buy it for my office because I'd never get anything done. It *is* tempting, though."

I nod thoughtfully. "I see what you mean. This artist is from up in Astoria, and we feature many pieces from him here in the gallery. Take your time to think it over, and let me know if you need anything."

"Wait. Perhaps we should talk it over more, maybe over lunch?"

She bites her lip provocatively, and I want to roll my eyes, which is rude and unkind, so I simply smile but shake my head. "I'm sorry, I have commitments here. Spend some time with the art, and I'll be around if you have questions."

I nod politely and walk away from her. I'm simply not interested.

All I can think about is Sarah and the fact that she's moving into my guesthouse right about now. Or sometime today, anyway. I want to be there to help her settle in, and just to be with her, which just sounds creepy as fuck, even to my own ears.

I sounded so confident when I assured her that it would be uncomplicated to live so close to each other, but it's not that simple at all. Not for me.

Because despite my better judgment, I still have feelings for the woman that stole my heart at just sixteen years old. She was pretty as a young woman, but now she's *gorgeous*. Smart. Witty.

And although she hasn't come right out and said it, I suspect that a romantic entanglement is the last thing that Sarah wants after a bad marriage. I've given her space since she arrived home last year. Space to heal, to plant her roots here, and to get her equilibrium.

It hasn't been easy. At one time in our lives, I wouldn't have hesitated in reaching out to touch her to get her to talk to me.

We were as close and intimate as two people could get.

I was in love with her.

But, I was young and stupid, and because of hormones, I lost her.

Now, she's back in my life, and as of this afternoon, she'll be living about ten yards away from me.

"I'm an idiot," I mutter before pushing my hand through my hair. How do I sleep mere feet away from her? I won't, that's how, because I'll yearn to be in that bed with her, listening to the ocean as I make love to her. I'm a patient man, but even I'm not *that* patient. "Idiot."

The bell over the door rings, and I see the back of the flirty woman as she walks out of it, and I'm not sorry to see her go.

I wander back to the painting that the customer was looking at and sigh. I've always pictured this hanging above the couch in the living room of the guesthouse, but I just never took the time to put it there. Sarah would love it.

She's always been obsessed with the beach.

"I'll take her any way I can get her," I finally admit to myself. If that means that we're just friends, and I make her feel welcome and comfortable in her new home, with no strings attached, then so be it.

Because although she's never confided in me about what happened in her marriage, I can feel that she's recovering from something bad.

And I'll be damned if I give her even *one* minute of uncertainty while she's living under my roof. I know what her childhood was like, so this part of her life will be exactly what she wants, on *her* terms.

She's earned that.

With a new plan in my mind, I take the painting from the wall and signal to Wayne, my assistant.

"Did she buy it?" he asks as he approaches.

"No, I did. I have some errands to run, but I'll be back in a couple of hours. Just call me if you need anything."

"It's pretty chill in here today," he says, glancing around. "Need help with that?"

"I've got it. Thanks, Wayne."

Thirty minutes later, I walk into the guesthouse, relieved to see that Sarah hasn't been here yet. It doesn't take long for me to hang the painting above the couch, and then I get to work on the rest of my plan.

I stock the fridge and freezer, fill a fruit basket for the table, and put a bouquet of flowers in a vase.

"Delivery."

I glance over at the open doorway and grin at Montana Jericho, the owner of Huckleberry Delight.

"You have impeccable timing."

She grins, a dimple flashing in her left cheek. "I know. One dozen lemon cupcakes with whipped strawberry frosting. Where do you want them?"

"Just here on the counter."

Montana frowns at me. "Are you going to leave them in the box?"

"Where else would I put them?"

She rolls her eyes. "I'll be right back."

I called her from the car and told her what I needed,

and why, and she assured me that she'd have the cupcakes to me inside of an hour.

She didn't lie.

Montana and I tried to date a couple of years ago. She's a beautiful, bright woman who runs a successful business. But after three dates, and one night of sex, we decided that we're much better as friends.

She hurries in, carrying a pretty cake stand. The base is made out of driftwood, and it has a handblown glass dome that fits over the top. She painstakingly arranges the cupcakes on it, then fits the dome over them.

"I'll pay you for that."

"You sure will." Her smile is bright as she winks at me. "I'll add it to the tab. It looks great in here. Sarah will love it."

"I just want her to feel welcome."

"I think you succeeded in that, and I love that you want it for her. Sarah's awesome." Montana pats my shoulder and turns for the doorway. "Have a good day, Tanner."

"You, too. Thanks, Montana."

I grab the simple card I brought with me from the gallery and write *Welcome home, Sarah. –Tanner*

Once it's leaned against the cake stand, I take one last look around and nod in approval before I let myself out, locking the door behind me.

This is one step in the right direction of making Sarah feel at home, with no awkwardness in sight.

"But I wanted to buy it. I *told* him that it was mine. This is absolute bullshit."

I frown at the shrill voice as I walk back into Whalers Gallery. The woman from earlier is standing at the counter, scowling at Wayne.

"What's up?" I ask as I approach.

"The painting *I* wanted is suddenly gone." She points to the wall where the seascape hung earlier. "I came back to buy it, and your incompetent employee isn't doing his job."

"I don't have any incompetent employees. Unfortunately, the painting you're referencing sold shortly after you left." I give Wayne a nod, indicating that I'll take care of this.

He walks away without hesitation.

I don't blame him.

"How is that even possible?" she counters, waving her arms about dramatically. "It hasn't been more than an hour since I was here."

"Like I said, it sold."

She narrows her eyes at me. "You're hiding it from me."

"I assure you, I'm not hiding it. I'm in the business of selling art, not playing games. I can see if I can get another print of that piece for you."

"I don't want a *print*, you moron. I want the original."

"And that has *sold*." Clearly, this woman isn't used to being told no. "I have other seascapes on the wall, if you'd like to look around, or I can find out if the artist offers prints of that particular piece. Otherwise, I can't help you."

If looks could kill, I'd be six feet under right now.

"Fuck you, and fuck this stupid, hick excuse for a gallery. I bet you would have been a pathetic lay, anyway." She turns and storms out of the gallery, and I let out a long breath.

"Well, she was pleasant," Wayne says as he joins me at the counter. "She threatened to sue if I didn't produce the painting. I told her I couldn't produce what I don't have, and she was welcome to contact her lawyer."

I grin at him. "Good one. I'd been meaning to buy that piece for my guesthouse, and after she left, I assumed she was passing on it. So, I took it home. I rented out the guesthouse earlier today and wanted to hang it before the new tenant moved in."

"Makes sense." Wayne nods. "I was going to hang the portrait of the train with Mt. Hood in the background in its place. It's the right size for the spot."

"Perfect, thanks."

My phone buzzes with a text.

Apollo: Beers after work. LP. 6:oo work?

I tap out my response. *I'll be there.*

It'll be a great distraction from thinking about Sarah.

"It's been a shit day." Apollo, my best friend of several decades, doesn't mince words as he sits on the high-top stool across from me at Lighthouse Pizza and sips the beer I ordered for him. "How about you?"

"It's been...weird." I sip my own beer, thinking it over. "Maybe Mercury is in retrograde or some shit."

"No, I think people just suck in general," he replies with a sigh.

"What happened?"

"I wired an *entire* house, over on Wildfire Lane."

"The rehab job on the big house that Genevieve Nelson used to own?"

"That's the one. The new owner gutted it, and to be honest, he probably needed to. It's an old house. So, updated plumbing and electrical, all that jazz."

"Okay."

"I finished up, and he says to me, 'I wanted electrical in the pantry.' And I said, 'That wasn't in the plan, but if you want that, I can add it.'"

"This doesn't sound too bad."

"He wants it for *free*. Because I should have known that he wanted it to begin with, and it should have been in the estimate. What am I, a fucking mind reader?"

"I assume you told him that it would *not* be free."

"Oh, I did. And he was pissed, and we exchanged some shit words until I just walked out on him. If he wants it done, he can find someone else. I'm busy enough as it is, and I don't need that shit."

"I got yelled at today, too," I inform my friend, and watch as his eyebrows climb in surprise. "I run a business, Apollo. It happens."

"In an *art gallery*?" He shakes his head. "Aren't

people supposed to be happy when they look at art? If they're pissed off, you're carrying the wrong stuff, my man."

"Ha ha. I'll have you know that some people take art very seriously. But yes, a woman came in..." I tell him the story, and when I'm done, Apollo's laughing into his beer.

"Ridiculous," he mutters. "Wait, who did you rent the little house to?"

"Sarah."

Our pizza is delivered, and I dig in, suddenly starving. Lighthouse Pizza has the best pie in Oregon.

"*Sarah* Sarah?" he asks and slips a slice onto his plate. "As in *your* Sarah?"

"She's not *mine*." And the reminder leaves a bad taste in my mouth. So much for not thinking about her this evening. "She wanted to move out of June's place, and it worked out well for her."

"Hell, who would *want* to live with June?" Apollo asks with a scowl.

I don't bother to say that the way he looks at June, the way he goads her and bickers with her, is so full of sexual energy that I don't think *he'd* mind living with her.

He'd probably punch me.

"I think it makes sense for a grown woman to want her own space." I reach for a napkin. "And this way, she can walk to work, and she has beach access. She likes to walk the beach."

"Uh-huh." Apollo narrows his eyes on me. "Perhaps there will be some hooking up. That, too, would be convenient."

"We're friends. Nothing more."

"I know you, man. And I know that you never stopped caring about her. She's here, has been for a while now, and I don't think it's a bad idea to make a move. If you keep waiting, someone else will move in on her, and you'll be elbowed out of the way again. Don't be a jerk twice with the same woman."

The thought of someone else with Sarah ignites flames in my belly. "Thanks for the advice, Dr. Ruth."

"That'll be five hundred bucks."

"How about I just pay for the beers?"

"Sounds fair. After this, let's go to your place. I want to see the situation. See if there's anything I can do. I like Sarah."

"I'm so relieved that I can bring entertainment to your life."

"Me, too. Aside from a bitchy homeowner, my life is damn boring."

"We could probably change that." I bite into the pizza. "There are women in town who would love to date you. One of the sisters at Three Sisters Kitchen, maybe? They're southern and hot."

"Nah, I like boring. It's easier. Far less drama."

"How's the inn coming along?"

"Faster than I thought. I figured Luna was nuts when she said she wanted to open a new inn by this fall, but as long as there are no major snafus, I think it could happen. It'll be a lot of work, but Luna's never been afraid of that. And June's working like it's her one mission in life."

"Those women are a force to be reckoned with."

"You're not kidding. Speaking of, let's go check it out over at your place."

I pay the bill, and we walk out of Lighthouse Pizza to our cars. "You okay to drive?"

"Since when has one beer rendered me incapacitated, especially after eating half a pizza?"

"Not since high school," I reply with a laugh. It doesn't take long for us to drive the short distance to my house. I pull into the garage, and Apollo parks behind me.

June's truck is parked in front of the guesthouse.

"Looks like we're crashing a party," Apollo says with a grin, and we walk over to knock on the door.

A few moments later, Sarah answers. Her cheeks are flushed, and she's smiling with so much joy, it takes my breath away.

"Hi, guys. Come on in." She steps back and gestures for us to come inside. "We were just getting settled."

"Meow."

Petunia ribbons between my legs and purrs when I pick her up and scratch behind her ears.

"She likes you," Sarah says with surprise.

"I'm a likable guy."

"Ugh, why are *you* here?" June demands, glaring at Apollo.

"We heard there was a creep in the area and decided to check it out. Turns out, the rumor was true, because here you are," Apollo says to June with a satisfied grin.

"You're so fucking witty," June says with a roll of the eyes.

"I know. Nice digs, Sarah."

"Isn't it awesome?" she gushes as she looks around the space with flushed cheeks. "It's a little cramped with all of us in here, but as summer gets closer, I can use the back patio as entertaining space, too, so Luna isn't always the one to host our fun dinners. And look, I have space for a studio!"

She shows us into the small nook that the last tenant used as an office, and I lean against the wall, watching as Sarah points out all of her ideas.

I love that she's going to make art here.

"But the best part is, I can see the ocean from here. And it's just a short walk down to the beach. I'll probably walk down there every morning."

"Thank you," Luna says quietly beside me. "She's stupidly happy."

"She should always be happy."

I feel Luna look up at me, so I meet her gaze.

"Does she know?" she asks.

"About what?"

"That you're still in love with her?"

My eyes turn back to Sarah, who's joking with June and Apollo. Her head is tossed back, and she's laughing.

I want to kiss her neck.

"No. And she may not for a long while."

"Oh, Tanner. Don't be too patient, okay?" Luna pats my arm, and we all turn as Luna's fiancé, Wolfe, walks through the door.

"I found you. Hey, this is cute. It suits you, Sarah."

"Are you mad that I'm not waiting for the apartment

above the garage to be done?" she asks and worries her bottom lip between her teeth nervously.

"It could be another year," he says with a sigh. "You'd be crazy to wait. We'll figure out something to do with it. Don't worry. This is way better. Quieter. And closer to your job."

"Exactly," Sarah says, excited all over again. "Petunia already found a sunny spot on the living room rug, and it just *feels* right here, you know?"

Suddenly, she turns to me and presses her finger into my chest.

"You didn't have to fill my fridge and leave cupcakes for me."

"Maybe it was the cupcake faerie?" I feel my lips twitch as her gorgeous eyes narrow.

"Thank you. It was the sweetest, and they were delicious."

"Hold up," Apollo says. "You ate *all* the cupcakes already?"

"Of course, we did," June replies with a satisfied Cheshire grin. "Too bad, so sad."

"You're mean," Apollo says to her.

"You're slower than I thought if you're just now figuring that out."

I want to brush the loose strand of blonde hair behind Sarah's ear. I want to pull her to me and kiss her until she can't remember her own name.

So, I take a step back and shove my hands in my pockets the way I always do when I'm around her, just to be safe.

"I'm glad you're getting settled. I'm going to head out. Have a good evening."

"We're about to go, too," Luna adds as I turn to the door. Once outside, I hear the door open and close, and footsteps sound on the driveway behind me.

"Tanner?"

I turn at Sarah's sweet voice. "What's up?"

"Thanks." She boosts up on her toes and presses her lips to my cheek. "Thank you so much."

"You're welcome."

Chapter Three

Sarah

"I'll be back in just a little while." I pat Petunia on the head, then scratch her under the chin before slipping my feet into flip-flops and pulling on a red windbreaker.

It's chilly on the Oregon coast in the spring, but I still want to feel the sand under my feet as I walk.

It takes me less than a minute to walk down the steps by Tanner's house to make it to the sand. Being near the water fills me with absolute joy as I slip out of the flip-flops and leave them at the bottom of the steps, then set off toward the surf.

The tide is way out, so I might find some shells or other little treasures that I can slip into my pocket and take home with me.

Clouds hang low, blocking the sunrise this morning, but overcast weather is nothing new here in Huckleberry Bay. And, although many people complain about the constant dreary weather, I love it.

I lived in California, in the sunshine, for far too long. I had no idea when I married Anthony and moved down there with him how much I would long for home. How much I'd miss my friends, my town.

My brother.

In the beginning of the relationship, Anthony made me believe that I could come visit any time that I wanted to. He was certainly wealthy enough that he could have made that a reality, but I learned right away that he never intended for me to come home, even to visit.

Anthony was a really good liar.

"He was too controlling to let me out of his sight long enough to come home to visit," I say out loud, not worried in the least that someone might overhear me. There are only a handful of other people on the sand, a runner and a couple holding hands, but they're far away, and the surf drowns out the sound of my voice.

It's one of the reasons that I love walking down here so much. My whole life, the beach at Huckleberry Bay was my safe place. My therapist.

"Because I can say whatever the hell I want, and no one can hear me. And it feels good to get it out."

When I was a kid, surviving my parents' bullshit, this is where I came to yell and cry.

When Tanner broke up with me, I came here to scream at the water.

And the night before Anthony took me to California, this is where I came to say goodbye.

"I was a fool." I lean down and pick up a rare shell

that isn't shattered to bits and tuck it into my pocket. "He swept me off my feet so fast because all I ever wanted was love. My parents didn't even love themselves, much less each other; how could they love their kids? Then Tanner left me. I just wanted to *belong* to someone."

I huff out a breath and stop walking just before the surf crashes around my ankles.

"And now, I belong to *me*, and that's how it's supposed to be. That's what I should have been chasing all along, rather than approval and affection from someone else."

I shake my head and let out a long, slow breath.

I need to go see my younger brother, Scott. He's the biggest regret in my life. I wasn't allowed to have any contact with him after getting married, and I wish I'd defied Anthony and maintained a relationship with Scott.

But, I didn't. I was weak and did what I was told to do. I just wanted to fly under the radar, and keep the peace, because to do anything else made my life a living hell.

And because of that, Scott hates me.

"I have to try to have a relationship with him." I wipe at a tear. "He's my brother, and I have to try."

Scott sought me out the night of the fire to make sure that I was okay, but since that night, we haven't spoken. I've told myself that I'm giving him space, but in reality, I'm nothing but a chicken.

"It's time to make things right."

With that decided, I check the time. It's not yet eight in the morning. I don't know for sure what Scott's working hours are as an EMT here in Huckleberry Bay, but I could find out by showing up to see if he's home.

So, I walk back to the steps where my flip-flops wait and climb up to my new little house. God, I love it here, more than I ever thought I could love a place. I enjoyed my little apartment above Wolfe's garage, but this is on a whole different level entirely.

The vibe of the space is calm and inviting, and it's so quiet here, I've been able to paint like a woman possessed since I moved in just a few days ago.

It feels like *home*, and I don't know if I've ever truly felt this way anywhere that I've lived. I certainly didn't feel welcome in my parents' house. My ex-husband made sure that I was never fully at ease when I was with him.

And the apartment, while comfortable and convenient, was above a busy garage, where it was noisy and bustling.

Finally, I have a place where I feel calm and utterly safe.

I pet Petunia and pour some food into her dish, and once I've rinsed my feet and dressed for the day, I walk the half-mile or so to Scott's house. Shortly after I returned to Huckleberry Bay, June and Luna told me that Scott had bought his own home and was doing well for himself.

I'm so damn proud of him.

I turn the corner of Cherry Lane and feel the butterflies set in. The last time I came to visit him, before the fire, it didn't go well at all. He said some hurtful things.

"It's been a while since then," I whisper to myself as I walk up to the porch. His truck is in the driveway, indicating that he's home.

Hopefully, he's alone.

I knock and step back, worrying my bottom lip between my teeth, and wait.

Just when I think that he's probably sleeping, and I should go, the door opens, and Scott frowns down at me in confusion.

"You okay, Sarah?"

"Oh, yeah." I clear my throat. "I'm fine. I just wanted to stop by and see you because I was thinking about you this morning, and...well. I just wanted to see you."

The last few words are a whisper, and he narrows his eyes, eyes that are so much like my own, and then steps back without a word, indicating that I should come in.

I don't hesitate.

"Your home is so nice," I say with a smile as I take it in. It's small but well-kept and modern. "It's a total bachelor pad."

"I'm a bachelor," he replies and crosses his arms over his chest. He's wearing his firefighter T-shirt and jeans and looks so handsome in it. So grown up.

Because he *is* grown up.

"Did I catch you right before work?"

"No, I got home about half an hour ago," he says. "I've been working nights. Listen, Sarah, I'm kind of tired."

"I miss you." I blurt the words out, stopping him. "I've always missed you, Scott, and I'm so, so sorry for everything."

He doesn't smile. Doesn't soften.

"I told you before that I didn't want to see you."

"I know." It comes out as another whisper, and I hate feeling this unsure, this *uncomfortable*. "I know you did. I just wanted five minutes to explain what happened."

"You got married and left me here alone, a kid, to deal with getting Dad's backhand on the regular. That's what you did."

I flinch as if he hit me because the words feel like a slap. "I know. Scott, that was *never* my intention. I had every intention of either taking you with me or sending money home for you. I thought that I'd be able to take care of you, but we weren't in California for even a month, and Anthony laid down the law. He said that *he* was my only family, and I wasn't allowed to even think about the life I left behind in Oregon. I begged him, but it was no use. It doesn't change anything, but I want you to know that it wasn't my freaking choice to abandon you."

"June and Luna took care of me," he says shortly, his voice laced with ice. "By the time I was in high school, Mom and Dad moved to Tulsa, and good riddance to them, and I got by. I did fine without you, and I still am. So, if you're here because you feel obligated, you don't need to be."

"I know, and I'm so freaking proud of you."

"No." He shakes his head and looks like he wants to

punch the wall. "*You* don't get to be proud of me because you didn't do a fucking thing to contribute to what I've accomplished. Based on where I came from, I should be in jail or dead at this point, and I'm not. I'm a decent person, who does good things for this community."

"I know you are. You were always a good person."

"Turns out, I was the only one in the family."

That stings, and I can't hold back the wince.

His hard face doesn't soften.

"You're right." I nod once. "You're right, Scott. I should have tried harder, gone behind Anthony's back, done whatever I had to do to make sure that you were safe. I failed you in that. I can't change it, and I can be sorry for it down to the marrow of my bones, but it doesn't make it any different; it still happened."

"I don't know what you want from me, Sarah."

"I don't want anything from you, nothing tangible, anyway. I'd like to get to know you again, and I'd like to be your friend."

"I have a lot of friends already, but if anyone dies, and a slot opens up, I'll be sure to let you know."

I can only blink at him, shocked. Did he really just say that? Scott doesn't look me in the eye, and anger just pulses off of him. I want to hug him, but I absolutely know that any touch from me would not be welcome.

I have to go. I feel the tears threatening, and I have to get the hell out of here so he doesn't see it.

So, I fake a smile and turn for the door. "Have a good day, Scott."

I shut the door quietly behind me and hurry down to the sidewalk and turn toward town. The further away from Scott's house I get, the faster I walk. This was a horrible idea.

I don't know why I thought that I could simply apologize and everything would be okay. Just because he was worried after the fire doesn't mean that he forgives me. It doesn't mean that he wants us to have any kind of relationship.

I'm not going to reach out to him again. Not because I don't want to, but because I just can't keep hitting this emotional wall, over and over again. It's painful.

I hope that one day, Scott will reach out and want to have me in his life. But he's an adult, and that's his decision.

I wipe away the tears on my cheeks and blow out a long breath.

"Enough of this. I have to go to work, and it's going to be another long shift." I walk right over to the diner and straight back to the break room where I stow my purse away in the orange locker with my name on it and loop a clean apron around my waist.

It's time to set my personal stuff aside and get to work.

"Breakfast has been busy," Angela, my coworker, says when I join her at the computer. "I have the right side of the room, so you take the left."

"Got it." I slip a fresh pad of order-taking paper into my pocket, along with a pen and a handful of straws. "Specials?"

"Banana bread French toast with bacon or a Denver omelet."

"Yum. Maybe I'll snag some of that French toast."

"I have a plate of it over there," Angela says, gesturing across the room. "Grab yourself a couple of bites. You'll need the fuel."

"Okay, thanks." I'm surprised. Angela isn't usually this *nice* to me. She's always been distant and kind of pissy in the past. But, I don't question it and set off to handle my tables. "Good morning. I'm Sarah, and I'll be helping you out today. What can I get you to drink?"

"This fork is dirty, I've been waiting ten minutes for coffee, and I don't think anyone wiped this table down before seating us here."

I look into the eyes of an impatient woman who is sitting across from a clearly embarrassed man.

"I'll replace the fork, I'm happy to pour you some coffee, and I'm sure the table was wiped down, but I'll do it again. No problem. Would you like coffee, too?"

"Of course, he does," she snaps, but I continue to look at the man.

"Coffee would be great," he says with a polite smile.

"Coming right up. Would you like to order now or when I come back with your coffee?"

"Since we've been waiting so long, we'll order now." She rolls her eyes, as if I should have known that already. "I'll have the Denver omelet with no onions, wheat toast, and the house potatoes."

"Got it. And you?"

"Wait. You aren't going to write it down?"

I blink at her. "You're having a Denver omelet with no onions, wheat toast, and house potatoes."

"*No* shredded hashed browns," she says emphatically. "I think you should write it down."

I narrow my eyes. Am I being punked right now? "I promise you, I understand your order."

"I'll have," the man begins, cutting off the comment the woman was about to give, "eggs benedict with hashed browns and an English muffin on the side."

"Great choice."

"You're not going to write that down, either?"

"Nope, I'll be back with your coffees." With a super fake smile, I walk away, drop their menus in the basket by the hostess stand, and tap the computer to put in their order.

"She looks like a prize," Angela says as she joins me. "That's why I gave you that side of the room."

"Awesome. It's going to be one of *those* days," I reply and blow a strand of my hair out of my eye.

"Good luck." Angela pats my shoulder and hurries off to refill coffee mugs.

I love all my coworkers. Willow and Sunny are my favorites, but everyone here is awesome to work with. Even when the customers are difficult, Sunny and Willow are upbeat, happy, and we have fun together. Angela hasn't been one of my faves, but she's not horrible, either.

I love it here.

I hurry over and fill an entire carafe with coffee, and

place it, along with the mugs, sweetener, and creamer, on a tray, and carry it over to Miss Difficult.

"I brought you your own pot of coffee," I say brightly as I fill the mugs and set everything on the table. "Your orders shouldn't take long."

"If you got them wrong, we'll send them back," she warns me, and reaches for her mug. "There's no Splenda in here."

"I'll grab you some."

I walk away and find the yellow packets, then return to the table.

"Here you go."

Before she can complain about anything else, I leave the table to greet new customers and get the rest of my day going. Things are moving fairly smoothly when the order comes up for Miss Difficult, and when I set her plate in front of her, she scowls.

"I *knew* you should have written it down."

"What's wrong?"

"Melissa," the man warns, but she ignores him.

"I asked for no peppers."

Now I grit my teeth. "No, ma'am, you asked for no onions. That's what you got."

"Well, I meant no peppers." She pushes the plate away. "I can't eat that."

"Melissa, you don't have a problem with peppers." The man rolls his eyes. "She's just mad today. Her meal is fine, thank you."

"Let me know if you need anything else."

I walk away and take a deep breath.

Looks like I'm not the only one having a bad day.

It's been a long freaking day.

I'm bundled up in a hoodie and sweats, my feet bare, sitting on the back patio with Petunia, enjoying an extra-large glass of red wine after a difficult day at work. The clouds above are fluffy rather than dark and angry, and it's pleasant out here.

Normally, I'd take this time to paint, but I needed to unwind first.

Shed all of the negative energy before I let it soak into my home.

Tanner drives up and pulls into his garage. Rather than going into his house, he walks over to us. He's so impossibly handsome it makes my stomach jitter. His white button-down is unbuttoned at the collar, and his sleeves are rolled to his elbows.

What is it about rolled shirtsleeves that makes a girl want to purr?

"Hey there," he says as he approaches. He takes in Petunia and grins. "You have your cat on a leash."

I glance down at her pretty pink harness and matching leash and nod. "Yeah, she likes to be outside, but I don't want her to run off."

"Has she run off before?"

"I've never given her the chance," I admit. "How was your day?"

"It was pretty good, actually. And yours?"

I pause and stare into my glass before lifting it to my lips and taking a sip. "It might have been the shittiest day I've had since coming home. Aside from the night my house burned down, of course."

His eyebrows climb. "What happened?"

I pet Petunia, who's content to sit in my lap. "Oh, you know. Difficult customers. No, actually, really fucking rude customers. One tried to get me fired today."

"What? What the hell?"

"Yeah, well, Gordy laughed at her and told her not to come back. Tourist." I shrug a shoulder. "The rest were just...rude. Maybe it's the full moon or something."

"That's interesting, because Apollo mentioned that he had a rude client the other day, and I had a woman come into my gallery that same day and cause a scene. There must be something in the air."

"Well, whatever it is, it can just blow right out of here. It's mentally exhausting."

"I agree. What can I do for you, Sarah?"

He shoves his hands into his pockets, the way I've noticed he does often. God, he's handsome. Tall and lean, with muscles for days and tousled hair that just begs for my fingers.

I've missed him. Everything about him.

"I don't think there's anything to be done. Unless you can give all the tourists a stern talking to, that is."

He smiles, and it lights up the patio.

"I'll see what I can do." He looks like he wants to say more, but he just sighs and starts to back away. "You have a good evening, Sarah."

"Yeah, you too, Tanner."

He walks into the house, and I lean down to kiss my cat.

"I love this house," I say to her. "But I think I under-estimated just how much it would hurt to be so close to Tanner, but yet, so far away."

Maybe it's time to stop fighting the feelings I have for him.

DECEMBER 24, 2001

DEAR DIARY,

Luna's mom is the best. I hate Xmas. It's the worst holiday. Scott always gets his hopes up that Santa will come, but I know he never will. He never has. We've never even had a tree in this house.

But Luna's mom invited us to their house, and she told me privately that she wants to do something special for Scott. I love them so much. They treat us like family.

So, Scott and I are going over there today, and we will stay through tomorrow. Mom and Dad won't even know we're gone. They don't give a shit.

I'm just happy that this year my brother will have a present to open that isn't handmade by me. I know he says he loves those presents, because he's the sweetest kid ever, but just once, I'd love for him to open something from the store, wrapped in real Christmas paper.

We get to celebrate a real Christmas! I'll let you know how it goes.

TTYL,

Sarah

Chapter Four

Tanner

With Wayne out this week for a family reunion in Boise, I've been busy. I have two other part-time employees, but no one knows the gallery as well as I do, aside from Wayne.

And that fact is always glaringly obvious whenever the man's on vacation.

I swear, he takes two holidays a year because each time he comes back, I give him a raise.

Smart man.

So, when I get in the car to drive home at the end of a long day at work, all I can think about is a cold beer and watching the basketball game on the TV so I don't have to think about *anything* for the rest of the day.

But, when I turn into the driveway, I see Sarah muscling her way up the steps of her patio, loaded down with bags of groceries.

She has to have a dozen bags in her hands, and as I

step out of the car, one of the bags breaks, and cans scatter everywhere.

"Crap," I hear her mutter in frustration.

"Need some help?"

Her head comes up in surprise, and her cheeks darken with embarrassment. "Nah, I've got it. Thanks, though."

I can't help but think how entertaining she is as I lean back on the car and cross my arms over my chest, taking her in. She's always been stubborn.

I'm glad to see that hasn't changed.

She bends over, giving me a full view of her ass, and attempts to gather the cans, but she still has all the bags in her hands, as well, and the cans fall out of her arms as quickly as she can pick them up.

When some tomato soup comes rolling down the driveway, and I stop it with the toe of my shoe, Sarah blows her hair out of her eyes and scrunches up her face in a whine.

It's adorable.

"Why aren't you helping me?"

I laugh as I pick up the can and walk to her. "Because you told me *not* to."

"Well, I'm dumb, and you're supposed to know that."

I take the bags out of her hands and wait as she gathers the items that fell, then follow her through the back door into her kitchen.

"You can just set those on the counter there." She gestures to the empty peninsula and opens the small pantry closet to put the cans away, then turns to start unloading the rest of the groceries.

I'm three steps ahead of her, already filling her fridge.

"I admit, you're handy to have around," she says with a grin and passes me a block of cheddar cheese and some butter.

"You know, you could ask me for help with the groceries, rather than carting all of those bags back from the store on foot."

She shakes her head, sending her wavy blonde hair moving around her shoulders in a way that makes me want to run my fingers through the soft strands. "No way. You are not at my beck and call."

"I don't mind being at your beck and call."

She narrows her eyes at me and puckers her lips.

And fuck if I don't I want to kiss her with everything in me.

"That wasn't my fault, smartass. The bag was defective."

"Are you sure it wasn't operator error?"

Sarah laughs and closes the fridge, gathering the bags and stowing them in the pantry. "Okay, okay. I might have taken on too much. Anyway, want to stay for dinner?"

Yes. Absolutely. I want nothing more.

"I don't know, it depends on the food. What are you having?"

"Well, I just went to the grocery store, so naturally I'm *not* cooking. I have tacos being delivered in about fifteen minutes, and I have plenty to share."

"Tacos, you say? I'm in."

"Want a margarita?" she asks as she pulls salt, tequila, and a bottle of mix out of the cabinet.

"Are tacos even tacos without margaritas?"

"That's my philosophy." She happily begins to mix the drinks, and she looks like a professional bartender.

"Did you work as a bartender in California?"

"No, I wasn't allowed to work." The comment was made so casually, so off-handedly, as if she said, *No, I've never been to New York.* My hackles rise. "But I like to mix drinks, and because Anthony entertained so often, and he left the drink mixing up to me, I'm pretty good at it. I don't have the best tools for it here. When I lived with him, I had an awesome set that he had to have paid a mint for. The bar was *impressive.* But then again, the whole house was because he was all about showing off for other people."

She stops mid-shake and looks over at me with wide eyes. "Oh, God, Tanner, I'm sorry. I didn't mean to say all of that."

"Why wouldn't you?" I have to make a conscious effort to loosen my fisted hands. I want to punch that fucker in the face. "It was a part of your life, and we're having a conversation, Sarah."

"I know, but it's..."

"Awkward," I finish for her, and she looks down into the glass she's holding. "That seems to be your favorite word with me lately, and I think we should clear it up right now. It's only awkward if we make it that way. You used to talk to me about everything and anything. We've always been good at that, and there's no reason that we shouldn't be now."

"But that was...*before.*"

"Doesn't matter to me."

"You look mad."

I take a deep breath. "And here I thought I was doing a good job of hiding the fact that I want to punch that son of a bitch into the next century."

She doesn't smile. She simply watches me with sober eyes.

"Any anger or frustration that I feel isn't directed at you. It's maddening to know that you were mistreated for so many years, and there's absolutely nothing I can do now to change it. I can't go back in time and make it right for you."

"I don't need you to change it," she replies, surprising me. Her voice is firm, her eyes direct, as she continues. "I appreciate the gesture, but it's done. Finished. I learned a lot, and most importantly, I survived it. And I'm doing a hell of a lot better than I was when I first got home. I don't even feel like the same person anymore."

"I can see that." I can't help myself, I reach out to cup her cheek in my hand, and she leans into my touch. "I know you've come a long way in the past few months. You're a strong woman, Sarah."

"I am now." She offers me a soft smile just as there's a knock on the back door. "And there are the tacos. Thank goodness, I'm starving."

She hurries over to open the door, takes the bag of food, and thanks the delivery person before returning to the kitchen counter and sets the bag down. She pulls out six tacos, a bag of chips and queso, and paper plates from the pantry.

"You did buy a ton of food." I pop a chip into my mouth. "Am I about to eat tomorrow's lunch?"

"Nah, I'll grab something at the diner. I'd rather have the company," she says and leads me into the living room. She sits on the floor, her back against the couch, and I follow suit, sitting directly across from her. "So, who have you been dating since I saw you last?"

I choke on a chip, and Sarah laughs as I take a sip of my margarita.

"That's a hell of a conversation starter."

"Well, I just figure if we can talk about *anything*, including my former marriage, it's only fair that it goes both ways. Go on, you can tell me."

I chew my taco and wipe my mouth with the napkin she offers me. "I mean, there have been a few dates here and there."

She raises an eyebrow.

"Jesus, talk about awkward."

Sarah laughs. "Oh, come on, you weren't a monk for a dozen years."

"No, but you don't need to hear all about it. There hasn't ever been anything very serious. A few dates here and there. I dated one girl that doesn't live here anymore for a few months, but she got a job in Chicago, and I didn't want to do the long-distance thing."

"No, you're not very good at that."

My eyes find hers. "No, I'm not."

"Well, at least you recognize it." She wads up the paper from her finished taco and sits back to drink her margarita, licking the salt off the rim.

I always had a weakness for that pink tongue.

"Is everything going well here in the house?" I ask her, changing the subject. "Are you comfortable? Do you need anything?"

"It's the *best*," she says with a grin as Petunia sidles up next to me and starts to purr. "We love it here."

"I'm glad." I pet the cat as she curls up in my lap, and sip my drink.

"Speaking of that, I have the money for the deposits and such. I just keep forgetting to give it to you."

"I'm really not worried about it, Sarah."

And just like that, her chin firms stubbornly. "It's your money."

"I don't need it," I insist. "Those fees are usually collected because I don't know the tenant. They're a stranger to me. You're not a stranger, and I know you won't stiff me on the rent or destroy the place."

"But, it's just *normal* to pay those things," she says. "It's how it works, Tanner."

"Are you telling me that you have a couple thousand extra dollars just lying around that you can hand over without blinking an eye?"

She pauses and frowns.

"I thought so. It would just go into an account, waiting to be refunded to you later. That's silly."

"You make it sound like I'm the bad guy here," she complains, and I chuckle at her.

"No, you sound like the stubborn *woman* here, and I'm explaining to you why you don't have to be. Just say thank you, Sarah. Use the money for something you need, or whatever you want, for that matter."

"Hmm." She swallows the last of her drink and sets the glass on the table next to the couch. "Thanks."

She stretches her legs out and bumps my foot with her own.

"Wanna go walk the beach?"

I glance at the dark window. "It's dark outside."

"That's okay. I won't let you walk into the water." She winks, and I frown at her.

"Do you often walk on the beach in the dark after you've been drinking?"

All humor leaves her face. "Actually, no. I just thought it sounded nice. Forget I asked."

She stands and I join her, taking her hand in mine. "The thought of you being hurt freaks me out, Sarah. I'm not trying to be an asshole. I just worry about you."

"I'm a smart girl," she says softly and looks up at me with those big eyes. "You don't have to worry."

She leans in, and I brush my fingertips over the soft skin of her cheek.

What I wouldn't give to yank her against me and kiss the hell out of her.

But we're *friends*.

And she's a tenant.

"Thanks for the tacos," I say as I pull away.

"Sure." She clears her throat. "Thanks for your help with the groceries."

"Anytime." I walk to the back door and open it, then turn back to her. "Sleep well, Sarah."

I walk to my house, resigned to another long night of thinking about the sexy woman sleeping less than a hundred feet from me, and how much I want her.

It's going to be a long night.

"*Proud Mary keep on burning...*"

I glance over at the stage, where Sarah, June, and Luna are singing karaoke, including dance moves, and grin over the rim of my beer glass.

The six of us are at Lighthouse Pizza. The girls have been singing, dancing, and doing shots.

"Corner pocket," Wolfe says, pointing to the pocket in question and takes a shot.

He misses.

"Shit," he mutters in disgust as Apollo circles the table for his turn.

"If he makes this shot, he wins," I remind him.

"Are you *trying* to piss me off?" Wolfe asks, and I grin.

"I don't have to try. You're playing like shit tonight. What's on your mind, man?"

Wolfe glances at the girls, takes a pull from the neck of the bottle of beer, and then sighs. "I've been asked to drive in a charity race."

I shake my head. "What did Luna say? Did she throw a fit?"

"I haven't told her."

My head whips around, and I stare at the man in horror. Wolfe had a *very* successful career as an F1 driver, but he had a career-ending crash last year. He moved home to Huckleberry Bay to heal and start a new life, and he fell in love with Luna.

Hell, they're engaged to be married.

"That's not going to go over well." I watch as Apollo lines up his shot. "She might throw you off the cliff next to the lighthouse."

"I'm pretty sure I'm stronger than her," he says and rubs the back of his neck. "Maybe. Look, I don't know for sure that I'll do it. I probably won't be given the medical clearance for it, but the thought is damn tempting."

"You miss racing."

"Like I would a limb," he confirms. "But I love her more."

"You'll do what's best for both of you."

The girls come bouncing over to us just as Apollo sinks the shot, and they retrieve their drinks.

"It's handy having you guys around to guard our liquor," June says and sips her gin and tonic. "We don't have to worry about any roofies from strangers."

"We're the only ones here," I remind her with a wink. "But, you're welcome."

"Looks like it's our game now," Apollo says to me. "You go ahead and break."

I arrange the balls in the triangle and feel eyes on me. When I glance up, it's Sarah who's watching me with a hungry gaze that I recognize from many years ago.

She grins at me and slowly sips her drink.

She's wearing a short dress with a low neckline that shows off her tits spectacularly.

And when I lift my cue to break the balls, she leans over across the table, giving me an even *better* view, and says, "Smear him, Tanner."

My eyes are pinned on her breasts. I can't help it. They're *right there.*

"Those aren't my eyes, you know."

I shake my head and try to focus on the table, but it's the worst break of my pool career.

Apollo sneers as he walks around the table. "You let a dame ruin your concentration."

"I don't know what you're talking about."

But when I return to my seat, Sarah's sitting there, and grins at me as I approach.

"I stole your spot," she informs me.

"I see that."

She tilts her head to the side. "You can have it back, if I can sit in your lap."

I lick my lips and smile down at her. "I remember when you tried that on me in high school."

"It worked."

"Yeah, it did. But I'm good right now. You sit."

She pokes her bottom lip out in a little pout. "That's boring."

"Come on, Sarah, we need more drinks."

June pulls Sarah away, and I'm left with the guys.

"Well, looks like Sarah's found her flirting mojo again," Wolfe says, wiggling his eyebrows.

"It's not like that. We're just friends."

"Listen, if that's what you consider *friendly* interaction, you and I need to have a conversation about the birds and the bees," Apollo replies. "That girl has been eye fucking you since she got here."

"I think it's refreshing to see the mischief back in her eyes," Wolfe adds. "She's not so sad or unsure."

"She's more herself," I agree, and watch as she laughs with the other two girls at the bar. "Hey, I'll be back. I need to run to the can."

"But it's your turn," Apollo calls out.

"Let Wolfe take it," I reply over my shoulder.

But when I turn down the hallway to the restroom, I hear someone behind me, and turn to find Sarah standing there, a happy smile on her gorgeous face.

"You okay?" I ask her.

"Sure. You?"

"I'm good."

I turn for the men's room, but she slides her hand in my back pocket and stops me in my tracks.

"I can't go in there. It's against the law."

I turn and smile down at her. "What do you need, pretty girl?"

Her face softens. "Aw, you used to call me that all the time. I don't know, I just wanted to talk to you without the others."

"About what?"

She leans in close to me, and I know without a shadow of a doubt, that she's going to kiss me.

So, I press my fingertips to her lips, and she scowls at me.

"Hey," she says against my fingers.

"I don't think that's a good idea."

Her eyes flash. "In case you missed it, I've been flirting with you all damn night."

"I didn't miss it." Now there's hurt there, and I feel like a complete moron. "Sarah, you've been drinking, and we're friends, and—"

"Forget it," she says and yanks herself away from me. "You seem to think that I don't know my own mind when I've had a little liquor. I've had *two* drinks, Tanner, just enough to loosen up a bit, but definitely not enough to lose control. I know what I'm doing, but I'll gladly go find someone else who *wants* to kiss me and *wants* my attention."

She turns to walk away, but I catch her by the elbow, whirl her around, and pin her to the wall.

"You think I don't fucking want you?" I press against her and brush my lips against her ear. "You have no idea how badly I want you, what I want to do to you. But goddamn it, I promised you that I'd be a gentleman. Not to mention that once I start with you, I won't be able to stop, and I refuse to be anything but mindful where you're concerned."

"No one's asking you to stop," she says. Her chest heaves as she breathes heavily and clings to me, her hands fisted in the T-shirt at my sides. "Damn it, Tanner, no one is asking you to stop."

Chapter Five

Sarah

I can't stop staring at his lips. All I've wanted all freaking night is for Tanner to kiss me. He was a grade A kisser when we were teenagers, fumbling around in the few moments we could steal away here and there.

I bet he's out of the stratosphere now.

"I can't do this here," he whispers and swallows hard, as if telling me no is killing him, which is good because it's absolutely destroying me. "Not here, not now, Sarah. Not like this after all this time."

"So, you're not turning me down because I repulse you?"

His eyes widen, he furrows his brows, and then he *laughs.*

Just tips his head forward and laughs.

"*Repulse,*" he mutters. "Sarah, I've wanted you since I was sixteen fucking years old, and that hasn't changed for one minute. But honey, we're in a public place with our friends, and what I want to do to you is absolutely *nobody's* business."

I bite my lip at the idea of what he might want to do to me.

I can't help it. I haven't had sex in a really, *really* long time.

And even when it was new, and neither of us knew what in the hell we were doing, having sex with Tanner was always *incredible*.

"Don't look at me like that." His eyes have narrowed on me.

"Like what?"

"Like you want to eat me alive."

I offer him a shy smile and shrug a shoulder. "I *do* want to eat you alive. And I decided to throw the idea of awkwardness out the window because it's only weird if we make it that way, and I'm done with it. I've spoken it into the universe."

He boops my nose with the tip of his finger.

"I'm glad because I definitely don't feel awkward with you right now."

"That's a coincidence, because I don't either."

"Oh, my God, *why* are all of you so freaking full of hormones?"

We both turn our heads at the sound of June's voice, and I can't help but laugh at the look of pure torture on her pretty face.

"I haven't had enough alcohol for this," she declares and stomps away, throwing her hands in the air.

"June has issues with PDA." I shrug and turn to walk away from him. "I'll go placate her."

"Sarah."

I turn at his voice and see what I've wanted to see on his face for what feels like forever.

Hunger.

"This isn't finished."

I feel the smile spread slowly over my face. "Definitely not."

When I return to the pool table, I can see by the humor-filled glances from my friends that June told them what she saw in the hallway.

"Hi." I try to sound nonchalant as I sit on a stool and pick up my drink. "How's it going?"

"Not as well as it is for you, apparently," Apollo says and earns a punch in the shoulder from June. "Hey!"

"I have no idea what you're talking about. Nothing even happened," I reply, and June snorts so loud, it wouldn't surprise me if people two towns over can hear her.

"Right. That's what I saw. *Nothing*. Tanner practically eating you alive is nothing."

"He absolutely was *not* doing that. Maybe I fell, and he helped me up like a gentleman. Chivalry isn't dead, you know."

"Maybe she had something in her eye, and he was helping her get it out," Luna adds helpfully, and I offer her a high-five.

"*Maybe*," June continues, "she wanted to get her face sucked off."

"Well, that's a delightful way to put it," I mutter into my glass.

"Given that she's a grown adult, it doesn't matter what she was doing in the hallway," Tanner says as he joins us and wraps his arm around my shoulders. "Nosy Nelly."

"I am *not* a Nosy Nelly," June counters. "I just happen to *always* walk in on you people when I absolutely do *not* want to. Do those things in private."

"You sound...jealous," Apollo decides, watching June. "I could help you out with that."

"When a blizzard blows through hell," June mutters before checking the time. "I should go home. I have an early start at work in the morning."

"I'll drive you," Apollo offers and pulls his keys out of his pocket.

"No, I'm fine." June tries to blow him off, but Apollo just shakes his head.

"You may not want to kiss me, but you will *not* drive home after drinking just because you can't stand the sight of me," Apollo returns darkly. "Don't be so damn stubborn, Juniper. Let's go."

June's face hardens, but she follows Apollo out of the restaurant.

"He'd better be careful," Wolfe says with a grin. "She looks like she wants to murder him in his sleep."

"When are they going to admit that they're hot for each other?" I wonder aloud, my head tilted to the side.

"I don't know why people say that," Luna says, shaking her head. "June is *not* hot for my brother."

"Oh, yes, she is," Wolfe says and kisses Luna's cheek. "They're both just too stubborn to admit it."

"I should go, too." I can't stop the yawn, so I don't try. "I have a long day at work tomorrow, as well. I wish Gordy could find more help. As it is, we're all working doubles right now. And I don't mind so much, because the pay is great, but I think we're all going to burn out quickly, and the summer isn't even here yet."

"When school gets out, you'll have more summer help," Luna reminds me. "Just a couple months left to go."

"That's true, and I can't wait." I stand and gather my purse, and Tanner joins me.

"Let's go," Tanner says, holding his hand out for mine.

"You guys didn't drink much," Luna points out.

"We have to get our girls home safely," Wolfe reminds her as we all walk outside after waving goodbye to the owners behind the bar.

Once in Tanner's car, we're quiet as he drives us home. Nothing is far away in Huckleberry Bay, but I enjoy the drive with the window rolled down and the cool ocean breeze blowing in on my face.

Of course, I had the ocean air in California, but it's not the same as the Oregon Coast. It's just not quite as magical.

I can't help but wonder if I'll be embarrassed in the morning by the encounter with Tanner in the hallway tonight. I don't think so. I wasn't lying when I told him that I've decided to shed the feeling of shame or uncomfortableness when I'm with him.

And I feel *so* much better now that I've let that crap go.

No, I'm not embarrassed at all.

Tanner parks and cuts the engine, but neither of us makes a move to get out of the car. Instead, we sit in the darkness, watching the stars in the clear sky in silence.

Until he reaches over and simply takes my hand in his, pulls it up to his lips, and kisses my knuckles so tenderly, it almost brings tears to my eyes.

"I thought of you often." His voice is soft, breaking through the stillness. "Do you know how difficult it is to live in this town, where all of our memories live, without you here? Even if we weren't together anymore, it would have been so much easier with you here, because I know that even then, we would have remained friends, and I could talk to you about stuff."

"I'd like to think that would be the case." I press my lips together. "I'm sorry, Tanner. For all of it."

"Let's be honest, Sarah, it was my fault. I was the idiot who broke things off and went back to college, thinking that I was free as a bird and could do what—and who—I wanted."

"How did that work out for you?" I can't help but glance his way, watching the cringe on his handsome face.

"Let's just say that I discovered what it means when they say, *if you water your own grass, it'll be as green as the grass on the other side of the fence.* I should have fed the relationship I had with *you*. It was great, and I didn't even know what I had until it was gone."

"You were nineteen." I squeeze his hand, then turn in the seat so I'm facing him. "You were a kid, Tanner. A boy, and it makes sense that hormones were raging, and it wasn't easy to be faithful when you were hundreds of miles away. At least you had the decency to break it off with me before you started something with someone else."

He frowns, still staring through the windshield. "It didn't occur to me to do anything else."

"And that's why you're a good man. You did the right thing, Tanner."

He turns to me now, scowling. "How can you say that? I broke up with you, and you married the next guy to freaking smile at you."

"Wow." I suck in a breath and let it out slowly. "First of all, I'm not stupid. Yes, I was young and flattered that an older, wealthy man wanted me, but if I hadn't wanted to be with him, I would have said no. I didn't do anything that I didn't want to do, and it had absolutely *nothing* to do with you."

"I didn't mean for it to sound that condescending," he admits, shaking his head. "I just meant that the rebound guy is the one you ended up marrying, and he was a complete asshole to you."

"How do you know that?"

His mouth opens and closes for a moment, and then he sighs. "It's a gut feeling. You came home without much of anything to your name after being married for more than a decade. You were sad, Sarah. You seemed so injured, more than from simply deciding to end a marriage."

"I think ending a marriage all on its own would be pretty damn sad," I whisper, but then I shrug a shoulder. "But you're right. It wasn't a good marriage, from pretty much the minute we left Huckleberry Bay."

"Then why did you stay so long?"

"If I had a dollar for every time I've been asked that question..." I shake my head and watch as an owl flies overhead and lands on the roof of my little house. "I'd forgotten about the wildlife around here. It's so cool. Anyway, in the beginning, I felt stuck. I don't have parents that give a rat's ass about me, and he was *excellent* at isolating me from my friends and everything I loved here. He had the money and the power."

"Aside from being a controlling asshat, did he hurt you?"

"He liked to hurt my feelings." The words come slowly as I think it over. "I think he got great pleasure out of making me feel small. But physically, he was careful never to lay a hand on me in anger. Until that last day when he told me to leave, and I told him I'd contest the prenup. He didn't like it when I stood up for myself."

"What did he do?"

My gaze turns to his at the hardness in his voice. "He smacked me around, told me I would do as I was told, and to get the fuck out. He'd found a replacement. You know, if he'd never kicked me out, and we'd just continued the way we had for all those years—with him cheating on me, and me pretending I didn't know—I don't think I ever would have left voluntarily. Mostly because staying was *easy*. But he did me such a huge favor that day. Kicking me out was the best thing he ever did for me."

"I don't know what to say to that. I'm happy for you?"

"You should be," I reply with a smile. "Because now, I'm home, and I'm renting your adorable little guest house, and I've decided that we're going to have sex."

He coughs, obviously startled, and then laughs. "Like, right now?"

"No, but soon. I think that's enough walking down memory lane for tonight."

"I won't ask you more questions about your marriage, because it's ultimately none of my business, except for one thing."

"Okay, what's that?"

"Is it final? The divorce?"

"Yes. He's firmly in the past, Tanner, exactly where he should be. And I'm moving on with my life, full speed ahead."

"Good. Good for you, Sarah, and I mean that, whether we have sex or not. Although, I do like that idea very much."

I grin as I step out of his car and walk toward the house. "I had fun tonight."

"Me, too."

I stop by the door and turn to him. "I'm not asking you in tonight."

"I didn't assume that you were." He leans in and

kisses my forehead, and I feel the touch move through me, all the way down to my toes.

It's delicious.

"Sleep well, Sarah."

He waits while I unlock the door and step inside before he turns and walks across the driveway to his own house.

And when I close and lock the door, and turn to find Petunia giving me the stink eye for being out so late, I let out a long, gusty breath.

"Holy shit, he's potent."

"You're sure you're okay out here by yourself?" Luna looks doubtful as we stand in the grand foyer of the inn where I have my easel and paints set up, ready to get some work done. "It's a big place, and even *I* feel weird when I'm out here alone."

"I want to get the vibe of it all," I assure my friend, excited to start painting. "I need to get started on these pieces so they're ready for the grand opening."

"That's still a few months away, at least," she says.

"Clearly, you've never created specific artwork for a special place." I wink at her as I tie an apron around my waist. "Trust me, I'm great here. I'm not scared at all. Rose will protect me."

"Okay, let me know if you need anything." She turns to leave, but then spins back around. "Oh, I've been dying to ask. Did you and Tanner do...*it* the other night after the pizza place?"

I laugh and shake my head. "No, we didn't. We talked for a long time, and then he went home. But I made it clear that I plan to have sex with him."

"Oh, well, as long as you're both aware of your plans." She rolls her eyes, making me laugh.

"What's wrong with having a plan?"

"It kind of takes the spontaneity and romance out of it, don't you think?"

"Not really. Now, leave me alone so I can work. I'll see you later."

"Good luck," she says before walking out the front door and shutting it behind her.

Some would definitely find the inn to be creepy, at least in the state that it's in right now. The shell is finished, with drywall, electricity, and even plumbing.

But that's it. No flooring, no paint, and certainly no furniture adorn the space.

It's big and empty, and even my breath echoes between the empty walls.

"Next time, I'll figure out some music," I mutter as I reference my notes for the first guest suite and get to work.

I've been at it for at least an hour, and feel good about my progress, when I smell the roses.

Luna's family property has been haunted for as long as anyone remembers. It's something that June and I were well aware of when we came to visit Luna as children.

Not to mention the many nights that I came to stay

with Luna's family when my own home life was just too bad to stick around for.

The Winchesters were more of a family to me than the two people who brought me into this world.

"Hi, Rose," I say out loud, and smile when I feel a light breeze blow through my hair. "I hope you're happy with what Luna's done with the old barn, making it into an amazing inn, where people can come to visit Huckleberry Bay and enjoy the coast."

Of course, I've never seen Rose, or been able to actually speak with her, but there have been plenty of times that I've smelled her over the years.

Rather than being afraid of her, she's like an old friend.

"I'm glad you're here," I say and blow out a breath as I step back from the canvas to take it in for a moment. "I like the greens and orange in this one. I know it's not exactly *seascape*ish, but I think it captures the mountains really well, and it'll fit in with the décor for suite number one. I wish you could give me your thoughts."

A door upstairs closes, but not loudly.

Not as if in temper.

"Thank you." I check the time and start cleaning up my brushes, tucking away my supplies in the bag I use for hauling them back and forth. "You know, I wonder if Luna would let me store this stuff somewhere here, rather than bringing them with me every time I come over to work. I'll have to ask her. Thanks for hanging out with me tonight, Rose."

But when I reach for the easel, it suddenly goes flying across the room and smacks into the wall.

"Hey, what's gotten into you?" I walk over, and reach down for it, but it skids out of my grasp once more. "Do you want me to leave it here?"

I prop my hands on my hips and scowl, and a door upstairs closes once more, slamming this time.

"What in the world? I'm going to go chat with Luna, but I hope you're not mad at me, Rose. I actually *like* having you around."

With that, I leave the easel lying on the floor and walk across the small field to Luna's house.

"Are you done already?" she asks with a smile when I walk into the kitchen.

"I was in there for more than two hours."

She raises a brow and checks the time. "That went fast. How did it go?"

I tell her about the painting and Rose. "It was like she didn't want me to leave yet or something. Really weird."

"Or she agrees that you should just leave your supplies here, and I'm completely fine with that. I'm sure there's a closet out there you can use, and if not, I know I have space here."

"Thanks, that's helpful. Especially since I don't have a car."

"Speaking of, I'll give you a lift home." Luna reaches for her car keys. "Unless you want to stay for dinner."

"Thanks, but I have a few things to do at home."

The sun hasn't quite set yet when Luna pulls into the driveway to drop me off.

"I'll wait here, make sure you get inside okay," she says.

"How chivalrous of you." I wink at her, then lean over and kiss her cheek. "Thanks, friend. I'll see you soon."

"See you."

I walk to the house and freeze when I'm about a foot away from the door.

I whirl around and run back to Luna's car as she rolls down her window. "What's wrong? Did you see a spider?"

"My door is ajar," I inform her and then swallow hard. "Luna, someone's been in my house."

NOVEMBER 20, 2007

DEAR DIARY,

Tanner just broke my fucking heart. He's home from college for Thanksgiving, and we met at Gordy's tonight for dinner, and I was so excited to see him! But he broke up with me.

He wants to see other people.

Which is code for he wants to fuck other people.

We've been dating for three years. I gave him my virginity; we have been basically attached at the hip for years, and he just dumped me.

I've stayed in Huckleberry Bay because of Scott. My parents are getting so much worse with their drug use and the abuse they put on my poor brother, so I've stayed close by still living in the same house, even though I'm eighteen, and I could technically move out. He needs me, and I won't leave him.

But maybe I should have moved with Tanner to college. He could go to school, and I could work, and at least we'd be together, and he wouldn't be so lonely that he thinks we need to break up so he can see other people at college.

Is he embarrassed of me? He never has been before, but maybe he is.

I don't know what I'm supposed to do without him in my life. Besides June and Luna, he's been everything to me for so long. How am I supposed to move on without him?

We were supposed to get married and leave IIB with Scott and live a normal life together.

But now we're not.

And I don't know what to do about it. I guess there's nothing to do about it. I'm not some psycho girl who's going to chase him down and make him love me.

But man, I wish I could make him love me. I wonder if there are witches nearby like in Practical Magic *who can put a spell on him.*

Probably. But that would be wrong, too.

I want him to want me because he really wants me. God, I just want someone to love me! Why am I so unlovable? What's wrong with me?

TTYL,

Sarah

Chapter Six

Tanner

This is the first quiet night I've had at home in...I don't remember when. It's a gorgeous spring evening, and I have the accordion glass doors open to the outside, letting in the ocean breeze as I cook in the nearby kitchen.

The indoor/outdoor space is what sold me on this house a couple of years ago. Granted, I can't use it year-round, but when the weather *is* nice enough to open it up, it's damn satisfying.

Tonight, I have a steak on the grill, with veggies and potatoes. I *like* to cook. I just rarely get the chance.

Not to mention, it's not ideal to cook just for one.

Maybe next time, I'll invite Sarah to join me.

There's a knock on the door that faces the driveway, and I wipe my hands on my towel as I walk over to answer it.

When I pull the door open, it's as though I conjured Sarah out of my thoughts.

"Hey. I'm making dinner. Wanna share a steak?"

"Someone broke into my house, and I can't find Petunia."

Everything in me braces as I take Sarah's shoulders in my hands. "What?"

Luna hurries up behind her, talking on her cell phone. "That's right, the guest house behind Tanner's house. Yes. No, we haven't touched anything, but we can't find the cat. Okay. Okay, great."

Luna hangs up and joins us. "I just got off the phone with June's brother, Cullen. He's coming right over to check it out."

"It's so handy having a cop in the family," Sarah murmurs and swallows hard. "It wasn't you, right, Tanner? You didn't happen to stop in for anything and accidentally leave the door ajar?"

"No, that crosses a lot of lines, Sarah. Come in for a second so I can turn off all of the fires I currently have going."

"We'll wait out here," Sarah replies. "It's okay."

"I'll be right back." I hurry away, leaving the door open, and turn off the stove, then run outside and pull the steak off the flame and extinguish the burners on the grill.

I don't need my house to burn down because I'm too busy figuring out what the hell is happening with Sarah.

When I hurry back outside, Cullen is just pulling up in his cruiser.

"Hi, ladies. Tanner," he says with a wave as he and his partner, Hawk, walk our way. "What happened?"

"I just came home," Sarah says and takes a deep

breath to calm herself. "Luna was dropping me off. I walked up to the door and saw that it was ajar, and then I ran back to Luna's car, panicked. While she called you, I poked my head in, just to see if I could see my cat, because she's a rescue and gets scared."

Her voice catches, and I slip my hand into hers, giving it a little squeeze.

"Did you touch the door handle?" Hawk asks.

"No, I just pushed the door part. I called for her, but she didn't come. I didn't want to go inside, in case someone was still in there."

"Okay, you all stay here, and we'll check it out," Cullen says, then turns to his partner, and they speak too low for us to hear as they approach my guest house.

"Maybe the wind pushed it open," Luna says as the three of us watch the police circle the outside of the building. "Maybe you didn't latch it when you left, and it just drifted open."

"I *always* latch it," Sarah insists. "I don't know what I'd do if Petunia got loose, and I couldn't find her. I'm too careful for that."

"It could be a million things," I assure them both. "We'll wait to see what they say."

Sarah's too nervous to stand still, so she paces around my deck. Luna rapidly taps the screen of her phone, I'm assuming, texting Wolfe.

"Wolfe and Zeke are on their way," she says. "I also texted Apollo, but he's on a job site where there isn't any cell service."

"You don't have to alert everyone," Sarah says softly. "Chances are, it's nothing at all."

But when Cullen and Hawk come out the front door of the house, I can see by the look on their faces that they're not super concerned.

Still, I'm suddenly filled with white-hot rage, and mentally make a list of everything I have to do in the next twenty-four hours, just to make sure that I keep Sarah safe.

"Found the cat," Cullen says cheerfully. "She's under the bed, hiding."

"Oh, thank God," Sarah says on a sigh. "That's the most important thing."

"There's no one in there," Hawk continues. "And we can't tell if anything is out of place until you come in with us."

"Let's go." Sarah immediately sets off for her place, marching with purpose.

Luna and I hang back. "It's already kind of cramped in there," she says. "They don't need us getting in the way."

"I'm installing security first thing in the morning, and until then, they'll stay with me."

Luna cocks an eyebrow. "You might want to ask *her* if that's what she wants to do."

I wipe my hand over my mouth in frustration. "She'll damn well do it, Luna."

Before she can argue with me, the three of them come out of the house, Sarah holding the cat firmly in her arms.

"Well?" I ask. "Is anything gone?"

"I don't think so," Sarah replies. "There's nothing out of place. They didn't toss my stuff around or anything."

"We got some prints," Cullen adds. "We'll run them, see if they belong to anyone that wasn't supposed to be here, but it looks to me like the wind pushed the door open."

"Impossible," Sarah murmurs, shaking her head. "I *know* I closed it tightly."

"Without a camera set up, we can't know for sure." Cullen turns to me. "Do you have cameras out here on this building? It might have caught something."

"Actually, I do. I haven't done the same for the guesthouse because I didn't want to infringe on the tenant's privacy, but there are about to be some changes there."

I pull my phone out of my pocket and bring up the security app. We spend the next twenty minutes combing through footage, and then we see it.

"There," Hawk says, pointing at the screen. "They tried to stay out of camera range, but those are tires."

"And feet," I agree grimly, and watch as feet walk around the car but then disappear.

"They're in there for about ten minutes," Cullen says when we see the feet return, get into the car, and drive away.

"Do you recognize the shoes?" I ask Sarah, but she's already shaking her head no.

"They could be on a man *or* a woman," she says slowly, leaning in to get a better look. "It's kind of grainy."

"It's just sneakers and jeans," I mutter in disgust. "She's right. I can't tell if it's a man or woman."

"Well, at least we know that it was a person and not the wind," Luna says brightly, and then deflates when we all glance her way. "I'm trying to look on the bright side."

"We have the prints," Cullen says. "And we'll monitor the area closely. It was probably random. You're tucked back in here, where no one can really see what's happening from the street, so it doesn't surprise me that you'd be a target, but we don't usually have much B&E in Huckleberry Bay."

"Just call us if you need anything else, or if you think of something that might help," Hawk adds before the officers walk to their cruiser and leave.

Just then, Wolfe and Zeke drive up and hurry out of their vehicle toward us.

"What did they say?" Wolfe demands as he pulls his fiancée into his arms. "Just the wind?"

"No," I reply, my jaw set in grim lines. "There was someone here. Right before I got home from work."

"But you caught them on camera, right?" Zeke asks. He's Wolfe's business partner and best friend, and has quickly become a friend to all of us.

I simply shake my head. "Not a clear shot, no. I'll have security installed tomorrow, including cameras. In the mean time, you and Petunia will stay with me."

Sarah's gaze whips up to mine. "Oh, you don't have to do that. I'm sure we'll be just fine."

"I wasn't asking," I interrupt. "Someone broke into your *house*, on *my* property, Sarah. You won't stay another night in there until I have the proper security in place. I won't risk you."

"I'm sure that I could stay with Luna."

I narrow my eyes, and without looking away from her, say to the rest, "Give us a minute, will you?"

"Sure." Wolfe leads the others away, and I lean into Sarah, speaking low.

"I won't touch you or do anything that you don't want me to do, Sarah. But I'll be damned if you're going to stay anywhere but with me. I have plenty of space for you *and* the cat. You're safe with me. And damn it, I want you here."

Her lips tremble, but she firms them and nods her head once. "Thank you. We'd love to take you up on that."

"Thank *you*," I reply softly, and turn to the others who are in a small group at the end of the patio. "Thanks for coming to help, everyone. Do you want to come in for dinner? I can order something."

"Starving," Zeke says with a nod, only to be hit on the back of the head by Wolfe. "What? I *am* starving."

"Please stay," Sarah says. "And will someone please go into my house to get Petunia's food and dishes? Her litter box?"

"Done," Wolfe says, and he and Zeke walk to the house.

"I'll text Apollo and June, let them know we're here," Luna says, her phone already in her hands. "Hopefully, Apollo has service now."

"This is great," Sarah says as she and Petunia follow me into the house. "It'll help me keep my mind off of it. I know you didn't plan to have a houseful tonight, so I'm sorry about that."

"Friends are always welcome here," I reply and get to work putting away the food I'd drug out to cook.

The steak, I discover, sat in the heat too long, and is a lost cause, so it goes in the trash.

"Let's order burgers from Gordy's," Luna suggests as she and the guys join us. "We've had a lot of pizza lately."

"That's the bad thing about living in such a small town," Zeke says. "We don't have a lot of food options. Also, holy shit, Tanner, this place is *stellar*."

"I've never been in here," Sarah says and sets Petunia on the couch before walking to the open wall of windows.

"The deck is totally closed in with a glass railing, so the cat can't escape," I inform her.

"This is something out of a movie," Sarah says as she turns to me with wide eyes. "It's so pretty. Of course, I've seen it from the sand, but I didn't realize that these windows were doors that open."

"We're going to have to have something like this when we build our house," Wolfe says to Luna. "We have to have it."

"I highly recommend it," I agree, and pull my phone out to place our food order just as Luna's phone pings with a text. "I'm going to order food."

"Awesome," Luna says. "Apollo just said he'll pick up the food on the way over."

"You guys are the best," Sarah says, watching us all with tears in her eyes. "I have excellent friends."

"We have to eat," Wolfe says, but winks at her. "And we love you, kiddo."

"I know. I love you, too." She swipes at a tear. "I want extra pickles on my burger."

"Extra pickles coming right up."

"You don't think this is extreme?"

Sarah watches as I screw a flood light into place above her front door.

"It's just this light, the camera on the front and rear, and the keypad with the alarm. Trust me, I could have gone *really* overboard."

"It was probably just random, and now that they see that I don't have anything worth stealing, they won't be back."

I stow away my drill and climb down the ladder.

"I won't take chances with your safety." I cup her cheek in my palm and lean in to kiss her forehead. "I should have done all of this before now. There's an app that you'll download onto your phone so you can monitor the cameras any time you want to. When you're at work, or even if you're in bed and think you hear a noise, you can look."

"Well, that's handy," she mutters. "Petunia might not want to come back here, though. She fell in love with that loveseat you have by the windows. She stared at the ocean all morning. Not that I can blame her, it's totally mesmerizing."

"I wish you had more ocean view out here." I want to suggest that they just move in with me, and call it a day, but I know she's not ready for that.

Someday, I'll have her in my house, and in my bed, all the time.

For now, she's just steps away from me, and that has to be good enough.

"I love my place. Someday, I'll have a full ocean view. But in the meantime, this is more than perfect for Petunia and me. Thank you for making me feel safer."

"You're welcome. Now, let's get the app installed on your phone."

"Right now?"

I stare down at her. "Of course, right now."

"You know, I'm not terribly technologically advanced. I should probably just muddle through it by myself later. It'll be far less embarrassing. This is my first smartphone."

"Oh, for fuck's sake, give me your phone." My voice isn't brusque or on edge. She knows I'm teasing her.

She bites that delectable bottom lip and passes her phone to me, and within seconds, I have the app downloaded.

"Okay, just put in your email and password here."

"But this is *your* house and your security. Shouldn't you have the account?"

"Absolutely not. It's your privacy, Sarah. If you move out, and another renter comes in, we'll delete your account, and the new tenant can set up a new one, using the same equipment. It's no big deal."

She scrunches up her nose for a heartbeat, and then, with her tongue between her teeth, she punches the information into her phone.

"Okay, now we're going to name the cameras, and make sure they're positioned the way you want them."

For the next thirty minutes, we get the entire system set up exactly the way she wants it to be, and then I decide that I'm not ready to walk away from her for the day.

"How about dinner at my place?" I suggest.

"I've imposed on you for almost twenty-four hours, Tanner."

"This isn't an imposition." I rub a lock of her blonde hair between my thumb and forefinger. "Let's call it a date."

Her eyes dilate, and she swallows hard. "I don't even know *how* to date anymore. I don't remember the last time I was on one."

"It's not hard. You see, I invite you over, you accept, and then we hang out together for a good amount of time. Then, before you go home, I kiss you. Sometimes, there's sex involved, but there doesn't have to be. Also, this way, Petunia can spend some more time at my house, watching the water."

"Oh, my cat is invited on this date, too?"

"Sure. It's a casual date." I smile at her. "What do you say?"

"That sounds nice. What can I bring?"

"I have it covered. You can help me cook."

She laughs and shakes her head. "That's one skill I

never learned, Tanner. I burn boiled water. I'm horrific in the kitchen."

"You never cooked?"

"We had a chef." She shrugs a shoulder. "I was good at going over a weekly menu with him. And now, I take orders and deliver food, but I do not cook."

I nod slowly. "Okay, so we're adding cooking lessons to tonight's agenda, then. Do you still like salmon with asparagus? Maybe some pasta in a nice cream sauce?"

"Who doesn't like that?"

"Excellent. Let's go."

I gesture for her to walk ahead of me, and when she does, my eyes can't stay off of her ass. She always had a fucking incredible backside. It fit perfectly in my hands as she rode me, and that's absolutely *not* what I should be thinking about right now.

"What's wrong?" she asks.

"Nothing. Why?"

"You just cleared your throat, like, three times. Are you getting sick?"

"No, of course not." I lead her inside the house and point to her cat. "Looks like she hasn't moved."

"I told you, she loves that spot." Sarah turns to me and tilts her head to the side. "But really, what's wrong?"

"I'm great. You're here, and I get to eat delicious food."

Her eyes narrow. "Uh-uh. I don't buy it."

"You." I lick my lips and then lean against the kitchen counter, staring at her. "I'm thinking about *you* in ways that don't involve a simple dinner or me keeping my manners in check when I kiss you goodnight. I'm thinking about the way your butt feels in my hands when we're naked and the little sounds you make when you come, and how much I've wanted you for more than a decade."

I take a deep breath and watch as her eyes glass over.

"But that's not what we're here for. Not yet. So, let's drop it and have a nice dinner because I'm starving."

I turn to the refrigerator, open the door, and stare blindly inside.

"Tanner." Sarah's hand glides up my arm, to my shoulder, and over to my neck. When it's halfway down my back, I turn to her.

"What?"

"There's absolutely *no* reason that we can't have dinner *and* sex. In whatever order you'd like."

Fucking hell, my system can't take it. I cup her cheeks in my hands and stare into her eyes intently, searching to make sure that she means it and isn't just saying the words because she wants to pay me back for my hospitality.

Not that Sarah would ever do that.

"Make sure you mean it."

Chapter Seven

Sarah

"I don't think I've ever been more sure about something in my life." My eyes drop to his lips, and I lick my own instinctively as his hands drop away from my face. "I've wanted you forever, Tanner. Since I was a kid."

His hands flex in and out of fists, as if he's restraining himself from touching me, so I take one of his hands in mine and bring it back up to my face.

"I *want* you to touch me. I'm not fragile or broken. I'm a woman, well aware of what, and who, I want."

"I don't think you're fragile, but you *are* precious," he says as his fingers move into my hair to brush gently. "And I don't care if that sounds cheesy."

"Maybe only a *little* cheesy." I grin and lean into him, and when his lips press against my forehead, I can't help but sigh.

Tanner always did give the very best forehead kisses.

His hands drift down my arms, to my hands, and our fingers link. "How hungry are you?"

"I can wait." I squeal when he lifts me into his arms and carries me down a hallway to what I assume is his bedroom. It also faces the water and is a total bachelor pad, with nothing on the white walls, simple black furniture, and a messy bed.

He tosses me onto the bed playfully, then jumps over me and crawls up my body, kissing his way to my neck.

He still hasn't kissed me on the lips, and I'm *dying* for his lips to be on mine.

Finally, his mouth hovers just an inch from my own, and I can't stand it anymore.

"Are you ever going to kiss me?"

"Oh, yeah," he whispers, his eyes pinned to my mouth. "I'm going to kiss you, sweetheart."

He drags his knuckles down my cheek, tips my chin up just a bit, and then he sinks into me, and everything else just melts away.

This man can *kiss*. Never too much tongue or lips too firm. Never too needy or sloppy.

Just absolutely *perfect*.

And he kisses me like his life depends on it. Like his only job in this world is to kiss my lips and drive me wild.

It's been more than a dozen years, and yet it feels like no time has passed at all as his hands move down my side, then back up to cup my breast. I arch up into him, yearning for more, and he obliges, pinching my nipple through the fabric of my shirt and bra.

"Naked," I murmur against his lips. "We have to get naked."

"We will." He nibbles down my jawline, returns to my neck, and his hand dives farther south and pops open the button of my jeans. "I remember every inch of your body, but I can't wait to explore and rediscover you."

"I'm not the same." I gasp when his hand drifts under my panties and cups me, making everything in me tighten with anticipation. My hands dive into his thick, dark hair and hold on as he takes my body on one hell of a ride, even with my clothes still on.

He'll destroy me once he gets me naked.

But what a way to go.

"I always loved this little birthmark," he says, after pulling my shirt up and revealing the brown mark on my stomach. "It looks like Kentucky."

I giggle, then sigh when he runs his tongue over that spot.

"They say that birthmarks are an indication of how you died in a previous life."

He pulls up and raises an eyebrow as he studies me. "So, what do you think this one means?"

"I was probably stabbed." I shrug. "But in a noble fashion, on a battlefield, fighting for King and country."

"Huh." He glances down at it once again and returns to kissing me. He peels my jeans down my legs and tosses them over his shoulder, then pushes my shirt up over my head, and I'm left lying here, just in my underwear.

And, miraculously, I'm not even a little self-conscious about it.

I reach for him, but he shakes his head.

"There is a zero percent chance that you're going to let me be the only one naked here." He smirks and gives in to me pulling his shirt off, then I climb up to my knees and reach for his pants.

"Fuck me, you're beautiful."

His words make me pause, my hands on the waistband of his pants, and I stare into his blue eyes. "You're distracting me."

"Sorry." His lips twitch as I finish the job of getting Tanner down to his own underwear, and then we're a tangle of limbs and tongues and moans as we tumble over the bed, hungry for each other in a way that hasn't happened for me since I was with him when I was eighteen.

The passion, the utter *need,* is palpable in the room as I finally straddle his waist, and his hands immediately cup my ass, squeezing just hard enough to leave a little mark.

I freaking *love* that.

I grind against him, and even through two thin layers of cotton, I can feel the length, the outline of his cock, and it makes me crazy.

I need him inside of me.

But first, I want to have a little fun.

"I know that look," he says, narrowing his eyes. "What are you about to do?"

"Relax. You'll like it." And with that, I move down his body, pull his boxer-briefs out of the way, and get to work on him.

"Holy shit."

I always loved doing this to him. His cock is smooth and just the right size. And the noises he makes, the way he grasps onto my hair, makes me feel like a goddess.

Suddenly, he jackknifes and slides me onto my back, moves over me, and spreads my legs wide.

"My under—"

My panties rip in half, and before I can gasp in surprise, his mouth is on me.

"Oh, my God."

Anthony never did this for me. *Never*. It's been a long damn time, and I come almost immediately.

But he doesn't stop. He adds two fingers now, and my head thrashes. I don't know if I can take any more.

"You can," he assures me. I had no idea I'd said that out loud. "Oh, you can, baby."

It's quite possible that Tanner has honed his skills over the past few years, and I want to sing hallelujah as he pushes me up and over another crest into oblivion.

When I'm able to open my eyes again, he's hovering over me with a *very* satisfied grin on his handsome face.

"Well, that was fun," I say. "As soon as my heart returns to normal, we can do other things."

"I think your heart's fine," he murmurs as he maneuvers his way between my thighs and rests his heavy cock against me.

But he doesn't slide inside. Not yet.

"Are you okay?" He brushes my hair off of my cheeks and kisses my nose.

"Oh, yeah." I swallow hard, catching my breath. "Doing good here. You?"

"I'm fantastic." He kisses me softly. "What's the birth control situation?"

"I'm still on it." I grin at him. "Got it covered."

"I'm gonna need an invitation here, Sarah."

"For what? Oh, *that*. I think the invitation is implied."

"Say the words." He kisses me again. "I want to hear them."

I raise my legs high on his hips, opening myself up to him. "Inside me, Tanner. I need you inside me."

His lips twitch again. His eyes are full of fire and lust, and finally, he rears back and fills me.

We both gasp.

I can't look away from him as he pauses, seated fully.

I clench around him and watch as his eyes glaze over. Finally, he begins to move, and he links his fingers around mine, pins my hands above my head, and freaking *moves*.

His muscles bunch and stretch, and I can only watch in awe. His body is so different from before, when we were so impossibly young. He's a *man* now.

And he's absolutely glorious.

"Ah, Sarah," he moans as he picks up the pace. I can't help but push my hands against his ass, and I can feel the pinnacle coming, faster and faster, until I can't hold back anymore, and I come apart.

Tanner growls against my ear and empties himself inside of me.

"I'M GOING to ruin this gorgeous fish." It's been thirty minutes since we rolled out of bed, and we're standing in the kitchen, organizing the supplies for dinner. "You should cook, and I'll sit this one out and watch. It'll be a learning opportunity."

"No way, you're not getting out of this one, babe. You'll be just fine." With his arms full, he joins me at the kitchen island, sets out a cutting board and knife, and grins.

Tanner doesn't have just *one* grin. No, he has several that he pulls out of his pocket for different occasions, and this one tells me that I'm about to hate whatever it is that he's going to tell me to do.

"I'm not touching that thing."

"Those are never words that a man wants to hear."

I laugh, just as my phone rings.

"Hello?"

"Hey, what are you doing?" June asks.

"I'm making dinner with Tanner. What are *you* doing?"

Tanner makes kissy faces at me, and I roll my eyes and turn my back on him.

"I have something I want to show you and Luna tonight. Can I pick you up around nine?"

"Nine?" I pull the phone away from my ear and scowl at it. "Like, in the evening? That's kind of late, isn't it?"

"You're such a grandma," June replies, and I can hear her roll her eyes from here. "I have to work late, but I won't have you out past midnight, I promise."

"Yeah, I can go out at nine. I might be in my pajamas and bunny slippers, though."

"Do you actually *own* bunny slippers?"

Tanner frowns my way, as if to ask what's going on, and I just wave him off.

"Hell yes, I do. I ordered them a couple of weeks ago. Hey, is everything okay, Juniper?"

"Oh, yeah, no worries. I just want to show you something, that's all. Don't worry about me. I'll see you at nine."

"Okay. I'll be ready." I click off and turn to find Tanner mixing something in a bowl. "June wants to show Luna and me something later. I have no idea what that thing is, but apparently it's happening at nine. Who goes out at that time of the night?"

"College students," he replies and sets the bowl aside.

"I'm definitely not that. But now I'm invested, and I have to know what she wants to show us. Anyway, what did you just mix up?"

"A lemon and dill sauce for the salmon. Don't worry, I left the fish preparation for you. I know you love that so much, and I wouldn't want you to miss out on your favorite thing."

"I'm not touching that dead fish." I cringe and shiver with disgust.

"To be fair, it's not a *whole* dead fish. It's just the filet."

"It's dead, and it's part of a fish. Ergo, I'm not touching it. You can't make me."

"Is it just fish that weird you out? What about chicken? Pork?"

"I don't like to touch any of it. But I can do it if I wear gloves."

"A-ha!" He points a finger in the air, then opens a drawer and pulls out some rubber gloves. "Here you go."

"Damn it," I mutter, but I put the gloves on, resigned to my fate. "Okay, what do we do?"

"Rub this sauce all over the fish. Pretend like you're giving it a massage."

"Not a chance."

"You're wearing gloves."

"You want me to give that fish a massage."

"It'll like it. It's a stressed out fish, and it needs a massage, Sarah." He laughs and demonstrates, sans gloves, how to do it. "See? Totally fine here."

"You can never touch me again."

He raises an eyebrow. "I'll wash my hands. Twice, if it makes you feel better."

"I don't think that's gonna work for me. You touched a *fish* with your bare freaking hands."

"What's this thing that you have with sea animals? It's dead and has no teeth, Sarah."

"I don't know, they just freak me out. They're delicious, but I don't want my hands on them."

"I guess it's a good thing that I never got that salt-water aquarium that I always wanted as a kid."

I wrinkle my nose, and Tanner busts out laughing, then leans in and plants a quick kiss on my lips. "Okay, I'll touch it, but you pay close attention."

"Deal."

"You weren't lying," June says in surprise when I hop into her truck, sandwiching Luna between June and me. "You seriously wore your pajamas."

"It's practically the middle of the night." I close the door and fasten my seatbelt. "Besides, if you can't handle me in my jammies, you don't deserve me in, well, anything else."

"I should have worn jammies," Luna mutters, which earns a scolding look from June. "But I'm dying to know what you want to show us."

"Me, too."

"It's something I've thought about for a long time," she begins as she pulls away from Tanner's house and drives through town, then turns away from the beach and drives inland. "I mean, don't get me wrong, I love living with Grandma, but there comes a time when a girl needs to move the hell out, and that time is coming. I can't move back into the shithole I escaped from, even if they *say* they cleared out the mold. I just don't trust it."

"No way," I agree.

"So, where are you going to move to?" Luna asks as June parks in front of the white chapel in the heart of the residential area of Huckleberry Bay.

Luna and I both scan our eyes over the houses across from the church. "I don't see any for rent signs."

"Not over there," June says, and when we turn our gazes to her, she points at the chapel. "There."

"You're going to live in a church?"

"Are you changing careers?" I ask, my words measured.

"No." June snorts and then gets out of the truck, and Luna and I follow her. "I *bought* the chapel, you guys."

Luna and I share a glance as we follow June through the gate of the old picket fence that surrounds the property, up the cracked sidewalk to the dilapidated porch that leads to the arched double doors.

June unlocks them, and we step inside.

"It's cold in here," I say, shivering.

June flips on the lights, and I'm surprised to see that it's mostly empty, except for two lone pews in the front of the big room. There's no altar left. The hardwood is scuffed, but still beautiful, and I know that June can sand it and make it shine.

"It's bigger than I was expecting," Luna says, her gaze thoughtful as she looks up at the stained glass windows.

"That's what *she* said," I reply, and we all laugh in hilarity.

"There's a basement," June says when we've quieted down. "And I could probably add on to the side here."

"June, there's a cemetery out back." I stare at her, blinking. "Like, your backyard is a freaking *graveyard*."

"I know. Look, the cemetery is closed to any new internments, and I have no plans to disturb the people at rest back there. I don't mind having a cemetery in my yard, if I'm being honest. I'll keep it tidy, and people can come pay their respects when they want to. I'll put up a fence between the cemetery and the chapel building, with a lock, so those who want to access the graves don't also have access to my house."

Her voice echoes in the empty room as we walk around in a circle, taking it all in.

"I *do* love all of the old stained glass," Luna murmurs. "Will it be, what, a studio?"

"No." June shakes her head, and a dreamy smile spreads over her face. "Haven't you seen all of the old churches that have been turned into private homes? They're *so cool.* I already know where I'll put the bedrooms, the living space, and the kitchen. I'll even have one and a half bathrooms."

"What if you want kids?" I blurt out and prop my hands on my hips. "June, this is really cool, but it's so *small* for a house."

"I don't have kids," she points out, not mad at all. "And no boyfriend. I'm not going to pause my life just because of what *could* happen. If I get married and have a half-dozen kids, I'll buy a different house. But this is a project that I'm just itching to get my hands on. I know I have a lot on my plate right now, work-wise, but I'll be wrapped up with most of it before the end of the year, and then I can shift gears a bit."

We're all quiet as we continue to take it in.

"I need this," June says quietly. "I need something for *me.* Please don't take this wrong, Luna. You know I love building the inn. It's a blast. But between that and my other jobs, not to mention all the work I do for

Grandma at her place, I really need something that's all mine."

"Hey, if you're okay with a bunch of dead people twenty feet from your back door, I'm thrilled for you." I kiss June's cheek and take her hand in mine. "How can we help?"

"I might need ideas for design stuff. And I could definitely use some art for the walls."

"You don't even have to ask," I assure her.

"Can I point out one tiny, little detail?" Luna asks.

"Sure," June and I reply in unison.

"Um, when you've moved in, and you bring a guy here, you're going to be having sex in a *church*."

The three of us share a look and then dissolve into giggles at the thought.

"I mean, Lucas Bradford and I did a lot of things in youth group back in the day," June says thoughtfully. "But that was a different building."

"Have you told Annabelle yet?" I ask her.

"That I was totally inappropriate with Lucas? Hell no, I didn't tell her. Although, she probably knew."

"No, about the church."

"I wanted to show you guys first."

"You said you've had your eye on it for a while?" Luna tilts her head to the side. "I didn't know that."

"It's sat empty for a few years. Not long enough to do a lot of damage, and yes, I checked for mold, but it sat for a little while. And every time I drive by, I think to myself, I could make that into the cutest house. Well, it finally came up for sale, so I snatched it up."

"It's an awesome idea." I turn in a circle once more. "Please tell me you'll keep the bell in the bell tower, and we can ring it anytime we want."

"Hell yes, the bell is staying."

"Awesome. Oh, and speaking of sex, Tanner and I are. Having sex, that is."

There's silence for a full ten seconds, and when I turn back to them, they're staring at me with their mouths hanging open.

"Is it really that shocking? We never could keep our hands off each other."

"It's...unexpected," June says. "But no, not surprising. Good for him."

"Hey, good for *him*?"

"Oh, yeah, he's wanted to jump all over you since the day he saw you standing in my driveway," Luna says with a grin. "The man has the patience of Job."

"Huh. How did I not know that?"

"You've had a lot going on, honey," Luna replies. "Well, we have some fun things happening, ladies. New jobs and weddings and houses and sex."

"I wish I were having the sex," June mutters darkly. "Huckleberry Bay is way too small. There's no one here I want to fuck."

Luna and I exchange a knowing look.

"Right. No one at all."

June scowls. "Shut up."

JANUARY 5, 2008

DEAR DIARY,

I think I met the man I'm going to marry. Yes, that sounds dramatic, but I don't care. His name is Anthony. He started out as a customer at the diner, and he always asks to sit in my section. He's been coming in for two weeks straight. He doesn't live here—he was here on vacation—but he says he's extended his stay just so he can see me.

We've been seeing each other every day.

He's so nice! And so what if he's older than me? I mean, sure, he's in his thirties, but I'm mature for my age, and Anthony says that age is just a number. I mean, I AM an adult of nineteen! I'm not a baby.

Anthony is just what I need.

TTYL,

Sarah

Chapter Eight

Tanner

"I'll be right back," I inform Wayne, and close the door of the gallery behind me. It's been a slow morning, and I need coffee.

Over the past week, since Sarah and I started sleeping together, I haven't been getting much actual *sleep*. But I'd have to be a complete madman to complain.

Because it's not a simple case of insomnia or stress that's keeping me up at night.

It's a beautiful woman that I can't keep my hands off of.

Sarah insists that she should still sleep in her little house, and she's moved Petunia back over, as well.

But we end up in either my bed, or hers, every single night.

No, I'm not complaining, but I'd rather she just moved in with me. I don't even need the income from the guesthouse, so if she wants to use it as a studio, I'm fine with that. I've almost suggested it a dozen times this week.

But it still feels too soon, and the last thing I want to do is scare her off.

I wave at Montana, who's just setting out her menu board on the sidewalk for the day before I walk into The Grind.

The smell of coffee immediately consumes my senses, and I sigh in delight. Daisy, the owner herself, is manning the order station with a smile.

"Good morning, Tanner," she says. "What can I get you? Your usual?"

"Yes, please. And let's add a scone today. I'm surprised you still have some left."

"You got it. How's business?"

"Slow today. You?"

"Same, hence the scones. Mostly locals, but it's just the calm before the storm. Summer's coming fast."

"You're not wrong. When that happens, and the tourists flood in, I won't have time to come down for a mid-morning coffee. So, I guess I'll enjoy it while I can."

"Exactly." Daisy winks at me, then turns to greet the person behind me.

I love living in a small town, where I know everyone and they know me. It wasn't always fun when I was a kid, and I thought I could get away with something without my parents being called, which was absolutely *not* true. But now, it's great.

The businesses look out for each other. There's no

competition here, as there are usually plenty of tourists to go around for everyone.

I grab my coffee and scone and turn to leave, when I see my friend, Indigo, wave me over to his table.

"What are you up to?" I ask as I sit with him and take a bite of my scone.

"Waiting for a client."

"Anyone I know?"

He shakes his head and sips his latte. "No. A woman from out of town is looking for a vacation home here on the beach."

"Ah, a part-timer." I nod knowingly. Huckleberry Bay has its fair share of people who own second homes here, and only come for a short time each year.

"I believe that's the plan, yes. Anyway, how are you? Still liking your house, or do you need me to find you something else?"

I grin at him. Indigo helped me buy my house several years ago. He's a great real estate agent.

But he's also always the salesman.

"I'm good where I am. It couldn't be a better fit for me."

"Did I hear that Sarah's been renting the guest-house?" He sips his latte innocently.

"You looking for gossip?"

He just raises an eyebrow.

"Yeah, she's renting from me."

"Is that all that's going on there?"

I narrow my eyes on him. "Why do you ask?"

Indigo just shrugs. "Listen, Sarah's a beautiful, smart

woman, and your relationship ended a long time ago, but you're my friend. So, I'm asking if there's anything there between you two before I ask her out on a date."

"I respect you asking." I purse my lips, staring at my half-eaten scone. "Yeah, there's something there. She's spent more time in my house than hers lately."

I glance up to find Indigo grinning at me. "Good for you, man. Good for you." His eyes dart to the door, and he nods. "Looks like my appointment just arrived."

"I'll leave you to it. Have a good day."

I rap my knuckles on the table and then walk away with my coffee and nibble the scone as I pass by a tall brunette that's all smiles for Indigo.

It shouldn't surprise me that someone would find Sarah attractive and want to ask her out. She *is* amazing.

Hell, she's *everything*.

I glance across the street, and it's as though I've conjured her out of my thoughts.

Sarah is backing out of the doorway of Books on the Bay, a stack of books in all shapes and sizes in her arms. She has a tote bag slung over her shoulder, and a bouquet of flowers peeks out of the top of it.

She looks like she's in a hurry. Her sunglasses slide down her nose, and she blows at them, as if the force will slide them back up again.

"Are you the heroine in a rom-com?"

She jumps, startled, and yells, "Shit!"

All the books fall to the ground in a jumbled heap, and Sarah stares down at them pitifully.

"Oops." I cringe and bend to pick them up, just as she

does, and we knock heads. "I think we really *are* in a movie."

"Ouch." She rubs her head as I squat and pick up the books.

"This is quite the eclectic collection," I say as I pick up each book, one by one. "Art, romance, horror. There's even a book on how to knit."

"I like all kinds of books," she informs me, and when I stand, she's smiling at me. "I'm going to have a bump on my head."

"Nah, we didn't hit that hard." But I lean in and kiss where she's rubbing with her fingertips. "What are you up to, pretty girl?"

"Errands," she replies and falls into step beside me. "I have an hour before I have to be at work. I won't be able to come over this evening, by the way. I'm working late. Angela had to switch with me again so she could take her son to the doctor this afternoon. Poor thing is really sick."

"It's fine," I assure her. "Although, I'll miss you tonight. What can I do to help?"

She smiles up at me and bats her eyelashes. "Will you take these books home for me? That way, I don't have to haul them all over town today."

"You bet."

"Will you also check on Petunia? I feel like I've been ignoring her a lot, since I'm not there much between work and being at your place."

"Just bring her to my house," I say before I can hold back the words. "She's happier there anyway, with her view of the ocean. She's the queen, and we're merely her subjects."

"Oh, I don't think—"

"How about this? I'll get a litter box and some food bowls, and she can just come back and forth with you. Is that okay?"

"Yeah." A slow smile spreads over her mouth. "Yeah, that would be awesome. We'd like that."

To my surprise, she pushes up onto her toes and presses her lips to mine in a kiss that isn't chaste, but also isn't indecent.

It's a sweet, familiar kiss that makes it clear to anyone watching that we're *together*.

And I'm just fine with that.

"I'm going to get going," she says. "I can relieve Angela early, give her a break."

"Don't be surprised if Petunia is at my place when you get home. She can hang with me this evening."

"Thank you." She walks away and blows me a kiss. "Really, thanks."

"Have a good day, dear."

When I walk back into the gallery, I'm pleasantly surprised to see several patrons strolling around, taking in the art.

Wayne's eyebrows climb when he sees the books in my hands.

"You went *shopping*?"

"No, I'm just taking these home for Sarah." I stow them on my desk in my office. "How are things here?"

"They picked up a bit," he says. "I sold a bronze sculpture."

"Awesome. I can afford to keep you another day."

He smirks. "Right."

WITH THE LITTER box and bowls set up, I walk over to Sarah's with her books and let myself in.

Petunia comes running.

"Hey, baby." I pick her up, and she cuddles right into my neck. "Aw, are you lonely? Okay, come on home with me. I just have to find your food."

I open the pantry door and retrieve her food, then fill up the plastic bag I brought with me before locking Sarah's door behind me and setting off for my place, with the cat and her food in hand.

As soon as I set Petunia on the floor, she scurries to the loveseat by the window, climbs into her favorite spot, and settles in to watch the sunset.

"It's pretty great, isn't it?"

Not surprisingly, she ignores me as I fill her bowls with food and water and then start making myself dinner.

Halfway into boiling pasta, my phone rings.

"Yello," I say as I tuck the phone between my ear and shoulder so I can stir the pasta.

"I need some help," Apollo says. "I'm trying to move some furniture here at my place, and I need an extra set of hands before I kill myself over here."

"Do you need me to come right away, or can I come after dinner?"

"What are you making?"

I laugh. "Chicken scampi."

"Do you have enough for two?"

"I'll add bread. Give me thirty to finish cooking and pack it up."

"Thanks, man."

I sigh and glance over at Petunia, who hasn't looked away from the view for an instant. She's too enthralled by watching the people walk the beach, and probably by the waves themselves.

"Were you once a beach cat before you were rescued?"

No answer.

Before long, I have everything done and packed up, so I head out to Apollo's place. He doesn't live on the water, says it's too much work to maintain a house that's constantly exposed to direct salt air, and he's right.

It's a lot of upkeep.

I turn onto his street and park in front of the little place he bought close to ten years ago now, and climb the cement steps to the front door.

"Hey, thanks," Apollo says as he opens the door. "For the help *and* the food."

"It's never fun to eat alone. Let's move furniture after food."

"Good call."

I follow him into the small galley kitchen and see that he's already set out plates and forks.

None of it matches each other.

With our plates loaded, we sit in the living room and dig in.

"You've lived here for a decade," I announce after looking around the space.

"Yeah?"

"And you haven't hung even *one* thing on the walls."

He shrugs one shoulder. "I'm hardly here. I've been meaning to hang something."

"For *ten years*."

"Not all of us are art experts, okay?"

"But most adults don't live like—"

"Like what?"

I chew my bread. "Like coeds."

Apollo takes in his house and shrugs again. "It's clean. That's really all I need."

"Someday, a woman is going to come into your life and turn it upside down."

"See? Why do I have to hang anything? Someday, someone else will do it."

"That's a great way to think about it."

When we've finished eating, Apollo puts the dishes in the dishwasher and then gestures for me to follow him.

"It's in here."

"If it's the size of Alaska, I'm gonna be pissed, man."

"Half the size." He laughs and turns into his bedroom. "I'm getting rid of all of this furniture."

"*All* of it?"

"Well, except for the mattress and box spring."

"Why?"

He tries to act nonchalant, but then he rubs his hand over his face.

"A family down in Newport had a house fire. Lost everything."

"So, you're giving them your bedroom furniture."

"Yeah." He shrugs. "Like I said, I'm hardly here. All I need is the bed to sleep on. I'm buying them a new mattress. They wouldn't want my old one."

"You know, you're a nice guy, Apollo."

"Let's not let it get out. I need to move this stuff out to my truck so I can take it down to them."

"All of this won't fit in your truck. It's going to take several trips."

He worries his lip and then sighs. "Maybe I should just rent a moving truck. That would be easier, and probably better on the bank account."

"I bet we could get a few people to come over with their trucks, and it could be a caravan situation."

"You think?" he asks.

"Sure. Let's call around, and see what we can come up with."

Twenty minutes later, we have four additional trucks on the way over, despite it being dinner time.

"June's on board," I announce as I hang up the phone.

"You called *June*?" he demands with a scowl.

"Well, sure. She has a truck. What is your problem with her, anyway? All you two do is go at each other's throats. Kiss and make up already."

"She's a difficult female," he mutters. "So fucking stubborn."

"And you're not stubborn." I smirk. "Right. Anyway, sounds like we'll have a bunch of help."

And I'm not wrong.

Four trucks, with eight pairs of helping hands, along with other furniture that they all want to donate, show up to Apollo's place inside of an hour.

"You guys, this is...*incredible.* You don't have to do this."

"This is just what small towns do," Luna reminds him as she stands next to June, who she rode with. "Not to mention, I had stuff that I wanted to get rid of. Now I know it's all going to someone who really needs it."

"Agreed," Harvey, the owner of Lighthouse Pizza says. "Let's get this show on the road."

In a matter of minutes, we have Apollo's furniture loaded into the trucks, and then we're off, driving the couple of hours down to Newport.

"What made you decide to do this right this second, and not early in the day on a weekend?" I ask Apollo from the passenger seat. "I didn't even hear about a house fire down there."

"It happened last night," he says. "I got a call from a construction friend down there, who told me about it."

"Did you know the people?"

"Not exactly." He clenches his jaw, and I turn to face him.

"Is this about a woman?"

"No. Hell no," he says, shaking his head. "I don't always think with my dick, you know."

"Okay. What kind of fire was it, Apollo?"

The muscles in his forearms bunch as he grips the steering wheel tighter. "Electrical fire."

Fuck.

"And let me guess, you did the electrical in that house?"

"Six years ago," he confirms, and it all starts to make sense.

"You don't know that it was something that you did wrong."

"Yeah, well, I don't know that it's *not* something that I did wrong. We won't know until there's an investigation. They might have had too many things plugged into one outlet for all I know, but it's a house that I wired, and it burned to the fucking ground because of an electrical issue, so, yeah, I feel obligated to do something. I'm not a rich man like Wolfe. I can't give them money, or hell, offer to build them a new house, but I can do something."

"They'll have insurance, man. Did anyone get hurt?"

"No. No one was home."

"Well, that's something, then."

We spend a good part of the drive in silence, watching what we can of the scenery as it gets darker and darker.

I shoot Sarah a text, letting her know what's up, and before long, there are signs of more civilization as Newport comes into view.

Apollo leads the other trucks to a storage unit where

a couple is waiting, and when Apollo gets out of the truck and walks over to them, they shake his hand and offer him smiles.

They're not angry with him in the least.

I hop out and join the others who have pulled in behind us, and we wait for instructions.

"We're just going to put everything in here," Apollo says as he joins us, pointing to the large storage unit. "Tetris-style. They have some more donations coming in the next few days, so we'll pack this stuff tight and try not to take up the whole storage space."

Less than thirty minutes later, the trucks are unloaded, and everything is packed neatly in the unit, leaving plenty of room for more donations.

"Thank you," the man says as he shakes all of our hands. "We really appreciate your kindness."

I notice that June smiles at him, and without a glance back at Apollo, walks to her truck, and with Luna in the passenger seat, they drive away, headed toward home.

It's late when I walk back into my own house. Sarah isn't quite home from work yet. I offered to come pick her up, but she said a coworker would give her a ride.

So, I sit on the loveseat next to Petunia, and wait for her to come home.

I WAKE up and immediately realize that it's morning. The sky is lightening with the sunrise, and someone draped a blanket over me.

I must have fallen asleep before Sarah got home.

And I must have been *out*, because I didn't hear, or feel, a thing.

Coffee sounds like the best thing since sliced bread as I stretch my arms over my head and yawn, then sit up and scratch my scalp, but then I see movement through the window, down on the beach below, that catches my eye.

Sarah.

Walking down to the sand for a stroll along the water.

I grin and push the blanket aside.

I do believe I'll join her.

Chapter Nine

Sarah

I'm so freaking tired.

With my feet bare, I walk across the wet sand toward the water and take in a long, deep breath. I couldn't sleep last night, and it had nothing to do with shenanigans with Tanner.

No, he was sacked out on the loveseat when I got home. But the kicker was, Petunia was curled up with him, and they were both snoring peacefully.

So, rather than wake them, I covered Tanner with the small quilt that usually sits on the back of the couch, and then I went home to sleep in my own bed.

Except, I didn't sleep.

So, at one, I gave up trying and decided to paint. Last year, I painted a piece for Wolfe and Zeke to hang in their garage as a thank you for letting me rent the apartment above. Unfortunately, it was also lost in the fire.

It's time to replace it, even if they won't be able to hang it for a while yet.

I stop walking to check a rock left by the tide and feel a little thrill when I discover that it's an agate. In my pocket it goes.

Oregon is famous for the agates that can be found along the coast. I discovered quite a few when I was a kid, but my mom threw them away.

Because she knew I enjoyed them. It was as simple as that.

Is my old baggage what kept me awake last night? I don't think so. I'm just restless. And as grateful as I am for my job, it's starting to lose its shine.

I'm standing at the water's edge, with the waves tickling my toes as it ebbs and flows in and out. The water is *freezing,* and despite the warmer spring weather, the water won't warm up. The Pacific is always cold.

At least, this part of it is.

But there are the adventurous people who don their wetsuits and windsurf, boogie board, and swim.

Personally, I'm fine enjoying the water just like this.

I hear footsteps behind me and turn to find Tanner walking toward me.

He has that sexy as sin half smile on his lips. The one that makes me want to just eat him alive.

Then again, almost everything the man does makes me want to eat him alive.

His jeans are rolled up on his calves, and he's in a light, gray jacket.

And when he reaches me, he immediately takes my hand in his and kisses it.

"Good morning," he says. "I'm sorry I fell asleep."

"You probably needed it." I walk into his arms and rest my face against his chest, taking another deep breath when he rocks me back and forth.

The beach is great, but combine it with Tanner, and it's exactly what I needed.

He takes my hand once more, and we set off, walking along the shoreline, inches away from the water.

"What were you thinking so hard about?" he asks.

"How do you know I was thinking?"

"Well, I couldn't see your face, but you were standing there, with your shoulders practically up around your ears, and tension in every line of your body. I know you, pretty girl. What's up?"

I bite my lip and look out to the waves. For several minutes, we just walk on the sand, hand in hand.

"I think I'm being stupid," I say at last.

"I highly doubt it." He laughs and squeezes my hand. "You're one of the smartest people I know."

"Well, it's silly. Because I have a really great life right now. My house is the cutest, my cat is the *best*, and I have amazing friends. Not to mention, I have *you*, so it feels really petty and ungrateful to be unhappy about anything in my life right now."

"Sarah." He stops me, and we face each other. "You're not silly or stupid or petty. And I know for damn sure that you're not ungrateful. If something isn't *right*, you have every right to speak up about it. What's bothering you?"

I press my lips together for a moment before answering him. "Last night at work was *hard*. And I'm not afraid of hard work. I can do hard things. And I don't hate the job."

"Okay, stop. What happened?"

"People are just...*horrible.* Mean to service workers. Rude. Not the locals so much as the tourists. And not *all* tourists, of course."

I break off when he just raises his eyebrows, and I let out a gusty sigh.

"I need the job. And *most* of the time, I like it. I love my coworkers. But man, there are just shifts when it almost sucks the soul right out of me. It left me unsettled, and I didn't sleep much last night, so that's probably why I'm extra moody about it all this morning."

"If you could do anything for a living, and I do mean *anything*, what would it be?"

I blink in surprise. "I haven't thought about that in a long time."

"So, think about it. What would you do?"

"I'd paint. If money was no issue and I could do anything? I'd make art."

His lips tip up into a smile.

"What is that look?"

"I don't know if you realize this, but I happen to *own* an art gallery. Why don't you give me a couple pieces, and I'll hang them. I'm sure they'd sell."

"I'm not ready for that."

I turn to walk away, but he takes me by the elbow, stopping me.

"Wait. I've seen your work, Sarah. If you painted

some seascapes, or anything for that matter, I *know* I could sell them for you. I won't even take a commission."

"That doesn't seem right."

Now his eyes flash with something that looks like anger.

"Are you always this resistant when people want to help you, or is it just with me?"

"I'm not trying to irritate you. Look, for a long ass time, *help* came with strings. So, it's an automatic response now to simply say *no thank you,* because I don't want to owe anyone anything. When payback time comes, it's usually something I can't, or don't want to, give."

"I don't want anything from you," he says, and I believe him. "And I get that it's a gut reaction, but if I offer to *help*, it's because I want to. Not because I want something in return. Unless..."

"Unless?"

He smirks. "Unless you had the inclination to show me your boobs or something. No pressure, though."

"Ah, sexual favors." I nod knowingly and then laugh. "For you? Not a problem."

"Think about it," he urges. "I'd love to hang your work in my gallery. It would be an honor."

"You're sweet." I step to him again, and his arms come around me. We don't speak for a while, but rather, we just stand here, wrapped up in each other, listening to the waves.

"Have you ever noticed that the water sounds like

music?" He begins to rock back and forth in a sweet dance that makes me smile against his chest.

"I've noticed." I close my eyes and soak it all in. The magical sound of the waves, the heat of the man I love against me, and the gentle rocking as Tanner dances me over the sand.

The water tickles my feet as his hand moves to my side, and then the other to my right hand, and we're standing in a classical dance pose, moving on the beach. I can't take my eyes from his as our bodies, pressed together from stomach to knee, sway side to side, in a slow circle.

"You're the most beautiful woman I've ever seen in my life." He presses his lips to my forehead, and I know without a doubt, in this moment, I've never felt so treasured. So loved.

So *necessary* to another.

It's a moment I'll never forget.

Suddenly, the waves crash farther up on the sand, engulfing us up to our knees, and we laugh as we hurry out of the way.

"Thank you for the dance." I take his hand as we walk back toward home. "It was a really great way to start the day. But now I have to get ready for work."

"Work? But you worked late last night."

I shrug a shoulder. "Yeah, well, I'm on breakfast duty this morning. Is it okay if Petunia stays at your place today so she can watch the water?"

"Of course. When I picked her up yesterday, she clung to me, as if she were extra lonely."

"Oh." My eyes fill with tears, and I'm immediately racked with guilt. "My poor baby."

"Hey, she's fine. Honest. I didn't mean to make you cry." He frowns down at me. "She's got the good life."

"I know." I nod and brush away a tear. "I just miss her. I don't get to see her as much as I should. Maybe I shouldn't have adopted her. It's not fair to her."

"Okay, you need to stop it," he says, shaking his head. "Petunia is as happy as it gets. Anyone can see that she's way better off than she was before you came into her life. I think you need a day off, pretty girl."

"I do." I blow out a breath as we reach the top of the steps near the house. "You're right, I really do. I think I have the day after tomorrow off."

"Sunday?" he clarifies.

"Yep. The whole day."

"I'm closed that day, too. I'd like to spend it with you. No plans, nothing crazy. Just *with* you."

"That sounds like the best idea I've heard in a really, *really* long time."

———

It's after my shift, and Tanner doesn't get home for a few more hours, and I really need to paint, so I head over to the lighthouse after work. Thankfully, June stopped by the diner this afternoon and was happy to give me a ride.

"You don't look so good," Luna says as she walks with me out to the inn. June dropped me off and left, on her way to another project, so I should have a little time by myself to paint without the work crew around.

"How do I look?"

"Tired," she decides as she unlocks the inn and lets me inside.

"Well, that's fitting, since I didn't sleep a wink last night, and I worked two back-to-back shifts."

"Yikes." She scowls as she watches me get my supplies ready. "Why no sleep?"

"It was a shitty night at work yesterday." I blow a strand of hair out of my eye. "And, honestly, this morning wasn't a lot better. People are just *rude* lately. Have you noticed that?"

She blinks and slowly shakes her head. "No, honestly, I haven't."

"Well, that's typical."

"What is?" She props her hands on her hips now and looks more concerned than pissed off. "Sarah, what's going on with you?"

"Is there a sign on my forehead that invites people to treat me like shit?" I set my brushes and easel aside and turn to my best friend, frustration bubbling through me. "Like, what is it about me that makes the people around me think it's okay to use me as a fucking punching bag?"

"I don't treat you like that."

"Not *you* or Tanner or June. I'm not talking about our group, but literally every customer I had yesterday treated me like a piece of shit. Wouldn't look at me, answered in short, clipped tones. One woman had the audacity to pour her fucking coffee all over the table because she said it was *cold*."

"Oh, my God, Sarah."

"My coworkers don't get that treatment. Not one of them, and trust me, I asked. Do you know that I went to Scott's house not long ago to try to talk to him, and he told me he was all filled up in the friends department, but if someone dies, he'll let me know."

Her eyes fill with tears, and I keep talking.

"My parents couldn't stand the sight of me. Tanner dumped me so he could fuck the girls at college, but in his defense, at least he dumped me *before* he started sleeping around."

"That's a bright side."

"And don't even get me started on Anthony. That man was *horrible* to me. At first, I made excuses for him. He had a demanding job, he was stressed out, if I wasn't so stupid, he wouldn't be mad. But that wasn't true. I'm *not* stupid! He just got off on hurting me, and I feel like so many people feel that way about me, and I want to know what I did to earn that treatment. What did I do to be last on everyone's priority list, and to be the one that takes abusive words and behaviors? I'm so fucking *over* it, Luna."

"Me, too." She brushes angrily at the tears and fists her hands. "I'm over it for you. It ends now, Sarah. If a woman pours out her coffee, you don't smile and offer to clean it up. You tell her to get the hell out of the restaurant. And if your brother says something like that to you again, you tell him to go to hell."

"That won't mend the relationship," I mutter.

"Who cares, Sarah?" She opens her arms wide, clearly as frustrated as I am. "Because *he* certainly doesn't. I don't care who he is to you, he doesn't get to speak to you that way. No one does, but definitely not him. You don't have an *abuse me* sign on your forehead, but you've also been afraid to stick up for yourself, and that has to end, too."

"You're right." I pace the foyer, pulling my hair back in a ponytail. "You're absolutely right. No more smile and nod for me. If I get fired because I demand respect from the customers, so be it."

"Gordy won't fire you." Luna's voice is full of confidence. "Not a chance. He loves you, and if you told him this was happening, he wouldn't stand for it, either. Did you tell him?"

"No. I haven't told anyone."

"I love you so much," Luna says, surprising me. She reaches out for my hand. "Like, *so much.* You're kind and smart and so damn talented. But if you have one flaw, it's that you don't ever think that you deserve to be treated well. You don't insist on it in your life. And you deserve it, Sarah."

"Why? Why do I deserve it? I stayed with a man who mentally and financially abused me for *years.* I abandoned my brother and my best friends. My community."

"And you came home and apologized, and in case you missed it, your community loves you. But all that aside, you deserve respect and love because you're a damn *human being.* Period. You're a person, and you have feelings. So, the next time some asshole won't look you in the eye, you say, *hey, my eyes are up here.*"

I snort at the idea, but Luna just raises her eyebrows.

"I'm not kidding." She narrows her eyes and gives me the *mom* look. The one that says, *you'd better listen to me, missy.*

"You're gonna make an excellent mother someday. You have the mom stare down pat."

Her lips twitch, but she still doesn't smile.

"I want you to promise me that you're going to start standing up for yourself because you know that you deserve better."

"I will." I swallow and nod, already feeling better. "I have to, because otherwise, I'm going to go crazy. We're not even in the heart of tourist season yet, Luna. It's not even that busy, and this is already happening. I can't go through a whole season of it. I can't go to work every day, worried and scared that someone is going to be mean to me, so I'm on edge all the time."

"No one can do that and stay sane. No wonder you're not sleeping."

"Do you know what occurred to me this morning?" Feeling moderately better, I return to organizing my supplies. "I was out on the beach, and I found an agate."

"You always loved that."

"I know. I still do. Anyway, I remembered that by the time I was about sixteen or so, I'd collected a good-sized jar, full of pretty agates. All different shapes and sizes. And one day, my mom barged into my bedroom, drunk or high as usual, and asked me a question."

"What did she ask you?"

My eyes find hers. "She wanted me to drive her to the liquor store so she could get more alcohol. And I said no. Dad was passed out somewhere, and he'd beaten the hell out of Scott that morning, just for funsies."

"God, I hate those people." She drags her hand down her face. "Like, *hate.*"

"So, I stuck my little chin out and I said, *'No, Mom. You've had enough. Just go to sleep.'*"

"And that pissed her off," Luna guesses.

"Oh, yeah. She saw my jar of agates on my dresser, and because she knew I loved those things, she grabbed it and hurried away from me, ran outside to the dumpster, and threw it in so violently, the jar shattered. She warned me that if I tried to jump in and get the rocks, she'd break my hands into tiny pieces, just like the jar."

"Hate's too easy of a word for how I feel about your parents."

"I'd been collecting them for *years*, and they were just gone, all because I didn't want her to get more liquor."

"No, it was because you stood up for yourself," she says quietly, and I suddenly smell roses filling the room. "It's because you took a stand against a bully, and you paid for it. And ever since then, you've given in because if you stand up for yourself, you might lose something that you love."

I stand in silence, staring at my friend, and feel the blood leave my head.

"You're right." I sit on the stool I use when I paint and swallow hard. "You're *totally* right."

"I should have gone to school to be a psychologist."

I grin at her. "I can't afford you."

"This one is on the house."

We stare at each other for a long moment, and then I blow out a breath.

"Well, I'm officially done being a doormat, all because my *mommy* was a bitch. No more, Luna."

"Atta girl. You've got this."

"Okay, you go away so I can work now. I'm feeling moody, so I think I'll do the stormy seascape for the south suite upstairs."

"Oh, perfect. I can't wait to see it. Holler if you need anything. I'm going to bring you some spaghetti in about an hour."

"Yum. Thanks. And not just for the spaghetti."

"You're welcome."

She winks, and then she's gone, and I'm left in the inn with my paints and Rose.

"Okay, Rose, let's do this."

"Hey, Sarah," Angela says the next day at work. She gestures for me to come talk to her by the computer.

"Hey, what's up, Ang?"

"I have an evening shift again tomorrow, and I have to go pick up my kid in Newport at about five, and I was hoping you'd cover for me."

"Oh." I start to immediately agree, and then I remember that tomorrow is my first day off in almost a week, and it's been the week from hell. "I'm sorry, I can't help you out this time."

"What? Why?"

"Because it's my day off, and I have plans. Sorry, Angela, you'll have to ask someone else."

"But, I already did."

And cue the guilt, right in the stomach. But, I *need* this day off.

"I can't help you this time."

"So, you're just going to let me strand my kid in Newport? That's pretty shitty, Sarah."

"No." I prop my hands on my hips and turn so I'm facing away from any customers who might hear me. "You can make other arrangements for your son. You *know* you can."

She blinks and looks away from me.

"I know that we've all been overworked, and you want a day off. Well, guess what, so do I. It's my sched-uled day, and I'm taking it. I *always* cover for you, Angela, so the fact that you'd try to make me feel like crap is pretty shitty of *you*."

And with that, I walk away from her to retrieve some meals from the kitchen to deliver.

It's a wonder that I don't drop the plates, my hands are shaking so hard.

I established with Luna last night that I'm *not* good with any type of confrontation, but I've also resolved myself to having my own back.

I can't be walked all over anymore.

"Here you go," I say brightly as I set the meals in

front of the family of four. "I'll grab you some ketchup and another round of Cokes. What else can I get you?"

"This looks great," the dad says with a nod, and he smiles up at me. "Thanks a lot."

"You're welcome."

I walk away with a spring in my step. That simple smile was all I needed to make me feel better.

It's so simple. I'm not asking for the world.

When I pass by Angela, she's not speaking to me, but that's fine by me.

"What's up there?" Sunny asks as she joins me in the kitchen where I'm filling cups with ranch.

"She asked me to cover her shift tomorrow so she could go pick up her kid from her ex in Newport. I turned her down."

"Good girl. She wants to go to a *concert* in Newport, and her kid is spending the weekend with her mom, right here in Huckleberry Bay."

I stare at Sunny for a full ten seconds. "You're kidding me."

"Nope, it's the truth. You take your day off and get some rest. Or bounce on that fine man you're seeing. Hell, do both."

"You know what? I think I *will* do both. I like Angela. I know that she's moody sometimes, but I thought she was my friend."

"Whoa." Sunny holds up a hand, stopping me. "She's a *work* friend. And that's not to say that those can't also carry over into real life, but I've been doing this job a long damn time, and I'm going to tell you something. Be friend*ly*. Be kind. Laugh together when you're on shift. It makes the days so much better."

"But?"

"But watch your back. Just because you get along well doesn't mean that you can trust her, or anyone else, to have *your* best interests at heart. I wouldn't do you dirty like that, but I don't know that I'd say the same about anyone else here, aside from Gordy."

"That's a good reminder. Thanks, Sunny."

"Also, if she flips you any shit, you let me know."

"Nah. I'll handle it. I'm no longer accepting any extra shit in my life."

"Good girl," Sunny says with an impressed nod. "I love it."

The rest of my day goes way better than the previous one. Customers are happier, and *I'm* in a much better mood.

Is it possible that I've been feeding off of the bad energy, and vice versa? Probably.

Tanner picks me up at three, looking sexier than any man should be allowed to in a blue polo and jeans, and when he takes off his sunglasses, he takes me in from head to toe.

"Trust me, I know I need a shower and clothes that aren't covered in food."

"I was just thinking that you look good enough to eat."

I smile over at him. "Well, thanks. How was your day?"

"Profitable. And now I get to spend some quality time with you, so it just got even better."

"You're very charming today."

He grins and pulls away from the curb. "You ain't seen nothin' yet."

JULY 4, 2008

DEAR DIARY,

It's Independence Day, but I don't feel very free. I think I've made a huge mistake. HUGE!

I don't know what to do. He won't let me call anyone. I can't speak to anyone.

And now that we're married, I can't talk to Scott.

I'm in trouble.

Sarah

Chapter Ten

Tanner

Despite looking *much* happier today, Sarah still seems exhausted. Her gorgeous eyes are heavy, and she has little dark circles under them. I have a feeling that she didn't tell me all of the details regarding what's bothering her, and that's okay. She will when she wants to.

But in the meantime, I'm going to do everything I can to help her relax and recharge over the next thirty-six hours or so.

I park in my driveway, and when Sarah looks like she's about to walk over to her house, I hurry to her side and steer her back to mine.

"I need a *shower*," she says, her voice just this side of whiny.

"And you'll get it. Trust me, I have a plan."

"You have a plan for my *shower*?"

"I do." I kiss her cheek, unlock the door, and usher her inside.

Petunia jumps down off of her perch and rushes over to greet her human.

"Hi, beautiful baby." Sarah picks up the feline and buries her face in the cat's fur. Her shoulders sag, as if in relief. "Did you have a good day watching the water? You're so smart. So pretty."

The feline purrs and rubs her face against Sarah's in ecstasy.

"I'll be right back," I inform them both.

I make my way to my en suite bathroom and start the shower, check that her clothes, toothbrush, soaps, and all the girlie things are ready for her, and then walk back out to find Sarah standing at the wide windows, the cat still in her arms, rocking back and forth.

"Your shower's ready for you, madam."

She turns and grins at me, then kisses the cat before setting her back on the loveseat.

"Awesome. Lead the way."

With her hand in mine, I lead her back to the bathroom.

"I took the liberty of grabbing a few things from your place, but if you would rather have something else, just tell me, and I'll go fetch it."

"This looks great. Those are my favorite pajamas."

"I know."

"It's, like, three-thirty in the afternoon."

"I know that, too."

Her lips twitch into an amused smile. "Isn't it a little early to be in pajamas?"

"Not really. I don't plan on us going anywhere, so we

might as well get comfy for the rest of the day. I'm thinking lots of food, TV, and hell, whatever else we come up with is in order."

"I kind of love that plan."

She boosts herself up onto her toes to give me a smacking kiss, and then she shoos me out of the room so she can take her shower.

"I could stay. Wash your back."

But she just laughs, plants her hand in the middle of my chest, and pushes me out.

"I won't be long," she promises through the door.

"Take your time," I reply and press my hand to the door before walking away to leave her to enjoy her shower and set the rest of my plan in motion.

"You didn't pull the stuff out of the fridge like I asked," I inform Petunia, who simply swirls in a circle and begins to bathe herself in the afternoon sunshine. "I see you're concerned about it. But no worries, I have it all covered."

I scored some brownies laced with caramel, along with salted caramel ice cream, from Huckleberry Delight, and I even hit up the grocery store to make sure I have all her favorite snacks around.

"She should have options," I inform the cat, who just continues with her bath.

It's a warm late spring afternoon, so I push open the accordion doors and let in the salty breeze.

The cat doesn't ignore me now. She rushes out onto the deck and sits in front of the glass railing with wide, excited green eyes.

"Here, I bought you a bed for out here." I set the fluffy, pink bed that I found the other day next to her, but she just hunkers down on the bare floor and blinks at me. "Yeah, that's what I thought."

"Are you having a conversation with Petunia?"

I turn to answer Sarah, and my tongue has suddenly cemented itself to the roof of my mouth.

Holy fucking hell, she's gorgeous. Her wet hair is combed but tousled around her shoulders. Her face is clean of makeup and dewy from the goop she uses on it.

And in those pajamas—shorts that have tacos all over them and a matching T-shirt that says *Let's Taco-bout It* —she's just—

"Why are you staring at me like that?" she finally asks.

"Because you're hot as hell, Sarah."

She snorts and then actually laughs, shaking her head. "Right. This isn't exactly a sexy look, Tanner, but you said I should get comfortable."

I cross to her and tip her chin up, drag the pad of my thumb across her plump lower lip, and examine her eyes.

They're better. Not nearly as shadowed as before, but there's still just a hint of it there.

"I find that just about everything you do is sexy."

"What if I belch?"

"Adorable."

"Steal the covers?"

"I have plenty of blankets."

"What if I only want to watch romantic movies with

absolutely *zero* action in them, and I want you to watch them with me?"

"Am I allowed to fall asleep during said movie?"

"Absolutely not."

I grin and rub my nose against hers. "I'll happily do it *and* make the popcorn."

"Wow, with extra butter?"

"You bet."

"Okay, I have one more, and it's the most important."

"Hit me with it."

"What if I decided that I absolutely *hate* college football?"

That one makes me pause. Sarah knows how much I love football, especially college ball.

But I shrug a shoulder. "As long as *I* still get to watch it, I can live with that unhealthy and unwise decision."

She snorts and then presses her lips to mine. She smells fresh and faintly of citrus with something spicy, like cinnamon.

"Feel better?" I ask softly.

"*Much* better." She goes in for a second kiss. "Thanks."

"If you don't mind, I thought we could have an early dinner out here on the deck, and then we can just snack later. I bought a bunch of stuff. We can even watch a romantic movie if you want."

"I was hoping for action," she says with a sorrowful sigh. "But if you have your heart set on romantic, I can deal with that."

I nip at her chin and then set her away from me and walk to the kitchen. "We'll watch whatever you want."

"What's for dinner?" She leans on the counter and then lifts her nose in the air and sniffs. "Are there *brownies* in the house?"

"Yep. They're for later. Dinner is hoagie sandwiches, and yes, I'll add potato chips to yours, which I still think is the weirdest thing I've ever witnessed, but hey, I'm not here to judge."

"People eat chips *with* their sandwich," she says reasonably and hops up onto the counter, swinging her legs back and forth. "Why not in it? It all tastes the same and goes to the same place."

"It's just not the order of things." I shake my head as I slice the bread in half and then turn to her. "What do you want on it?"

"Pastrami."

I blink at her. "I have ham or turkey."

She giggles and reaches out to tousle my hair. "I know, I was kidding. Turkey's great. Cheese is a given."

She lists off her favorite ingredients, and I get to work building her sandwich. When I set it in front of her, she grins and then smashes it down, effectively crumbling all the chips.

"Yum," she says after taking a huge bite. "Thanks. I'm going out on the deck."

"I'll be right behind you."

After putting the finishing touches on my own sandwich, I follow her outside and sit across from her.

"You put your chips on the side," she observes.

"Like normal people," I agree, making her smirk. "I like seeing you happier than you were yesterday."

"Yeah, well, me too. I'd had a shitty few days, that's all. Work stuff, mostly, but after a nice dance on the beach with the sexiest man ever, and a conversation with Luna last night, I felt a lot better. Today was a good day. I had a coworker try to pull one over on me, and I totally stuck up for myself. It felt good. She's pissed, but she'll get over it. Or she won't, but I don't really care."

"Good for you."

She reaches over and plucks a chip off my plate, then pops it into her mouth.

"How are *you*?" Her face is suddenly serious.

"I'm great."

"No, how *are* you? Not small-talk stuff. I've been so consumed by my own issues, I haven't checked in on you, and that's pretty shitty of me."

"I really am fine," I reply and reach across the table for her hand. "In fact, I haven't been this great in a long damn time. You don't need to worry about me. Also, I have some good news for you."

"I *love* good news! Tell me."

"Well, I have a client who comes in a couple of times a year. She's an excellent customer and is an art lover. She doesn't just buy for herself, but also for others as gifts."

"I like her already."

"Well, she asked me if I had any new watercolor work. Of course, I immediately thought of you. I explained to her that I didn't have anything at the gallery, but that I'm very close with a talented artist who works mainly with watercolors. She'd like to see your work. She'll likely buy several pieces. No rush, of course."

Her mouth opens and closes, and then she sets what remains of her sandwich down and frowns at me.

"Why did you do that?"

The lump in my belly forms. The one that always does when it feels like I've done something wrong where Sarah's concerned.

"What do you mean?"

"Exactly what I said. Why would you do that? I told you the other day that I'm not ready to sell my art in a gallery, and then you go behind my back and offer it up to the first person who comes sniffing along?"

"Whoa." I hold my hands up and shake my head. "You're overreacting."

"I am *not*." Sarah pushes her fingers through her still-damp hair in agitation. "This puts a lot of pressure on me."

"It puts zero pressure on you."

Now she stares up at me like I've just grown a second head.

"I just said that there's no rush. I mean that. She's not in a hurry. Listen to me," I insist when she turns away and stares out at the water.

"I think I've heard enough."

"No." My voice is firm now, surprising her into whipping her head over to stare at me in surprise. "You haven't. You told me just yesterday that your dream is to paint for a living. This opportunity isn't quite that yet, but you have to start somewhere. Do you think that I can look into your eyes and see how fucking unhappy you are and then sit back and do *nothing* until you decide that you're brave enough to do it yourself?"

"Fuck that," she says, this time surprising *me*. "This isn't about *you*, Tanner. It's me. *My* art. *My* time. *My* job. If I want to sell it, I will, and it's not up to you to decide whether or not I'm being brave enough to do it. Maybe it's something that I just want to keep for myself because it means something to me. If I choose to share it with the world, it'll be under my own goddamn terms. I won't be forced into anything just because you've decided to be a knight on a white horse and swoop in to rescue me. I don't need to be saved, Tanner. I'm doing great just as I am."

"Right." I nod and push my own plate aside. "You're right. I should mind my own fucking business. Except, spoiler alert, you *are* my business."

"Not everything I am is up to you. Isn't it okay, and normal, to have an off day? An off week? Hell, some people have an off year. I had a bad week, and it got to me. That doesn't mean that I have to *be brave* and turn my life upside down. I just got it flipped in the right direction as it is, and maybe I'm not ready for a big change right now. Not because I'm not brave, but because I need a little calm for a while."

"I shouldn't have said that. You *are* brave."

"Maybe you shouldn't have said it, but it's how you feel." She licks her lips and pets Petunia when the cat hops up on the table. "I kind of hate that everyone sees me as this broken, hurt woman when I've pulled myself up, worked a job, and I'm putting my life together pretty damn well. If you're not happy with where I am in my life, maybe we're not ready to be together."

And with that, she scoops up the cat and walks out on me, marching right for her house.

I hear her slam the door shut when she gets there, and I swear ripely.

"You're a fucking idiot," I mutter to myself as I clear the plates away and carry them to the sink.

I should leave her be for a while. Let her calm down.

I lean against the counter, and then decide, fuck that.

When I get to her front door, I knock loudly.

She doesn't answer.

So, I knock again. "Come on, Sarah, I want to talk to you."

She cracks the door and glares at me through tear-filled eyes, and it's almost my undoing.

"Hey, don't cry."

"Just go away, Tanner."

She tries to close the door, but I press my hand against it, stopping it.

"Please let me in, Sarah."

Finally, she just walks away, and I set off after her. The house isn't that big, so there's not far to go.

"I didn't mean to hurt your feelings," I begin and then take a step back when she whirls on me and advances like we're in the ring and a million dollars is on the line for the winner.

"You didn't *hurt my feelings*, you nitwit. You pissed

me off. I don't need you to decide what's best for me. I can do that by myself."

"You're right. You're more than capable. And I *did* see you hurting and thought I could swoop in and help. But, and hear me out here, the client would likely pay several thousand dollars for each piece, Sarah."

"I don't—" She stops. Stares. "You accidentally said several *thousand* dollars."

"No accident. And she'll be there whenever you're ready. There's no pressure."

"Felt like pressure, Tanner. Thank you for trying to help me. I know it came from a place of kindness and care for me, but—"

"Love." I shake my head and walk to her, no longer afraid that she might poke my eyes out, and cup her face in my hands. "It came from a place of *love*. Because I love you, and I want you to be happy. If that means that you want to work at Gordy's, great. If you want to sell art, cool. Hell, if you want to sit on my deck all day with your cat, I'm down for that."

"I hear the pay for that is really bad these days."

"I was a prick in my delivery back there, and I regret it. I'm sorry. You're brave and hardworking, and you're doing damn well without me butting my nose in."

"Yes. I am." She firms her chin, but her eyes have softened, which tells me that I might almost be out of hot water. "Please don't do something like that again, even when it's done with love. I don't want you to feel like you have to do things for me. But, I'm totally open to you doing things *with* me."

"I can definitely live with that. I guess I should throw away that letter of resignation that I'd written up for you to give Gordy."

Her eyes widen, and then she laughs. "I do love that you're a smartass. It's kind of fun."

I WAKE the next morning to Sarah's phone beeping with an alarm.

"What's that?" Sarah murmurs, still half-asleep and reaching for her phone, as I sit up and drag my hand down my face. "Holy shit, is someone trying to break in?"

"Not here," I reply grimly and yank on a pair of jeans. "Your place. You stay *here*. Do not leave this room. Call 9-1-1 and stay put. Promise me."

"I'll stay. Calling now."

I don't turn on any lights as I slink through the house to the back door and crack it open just a couple of inches so I can see what's going on out there. If someone is breaking in, I don't want to alert them that we know. I don't see any extra vehicles in the driveway.

But I do see a flashlight in the house.

Someone's fucking in there.

"What's happening?" Sarah whispers behind me, making me jump.

"I told you to stay put," I whisper in her ear and pull her back away from the door.

"I called the police, and they're on the way. Is someone out there? I don't see a car."

"No car, but there's someone in the house."

"Oh my God, Tanner."

I can hear the sirens down the block and rub my hand soothingly over Sarah's back. "Police will be here any second, and they'll take care of it."

There's a knock on the back door, and I don't even bother to tell her to stay put while I go answer it.

"Hawk," I say in surprise. "You guys work around the clock?"

"Shift work," he says shortly. "Whoever was in there is gone now."

"Impossible." I shake my head and step outside with him. "The alarm went off less than ten minutes ago. I saw someone walking around in the house with a flashlight. There's no way they've already left."

"Well, they did," he says grimly. "Left the door open again, though, and I'm hoping we'll find prints. There were none from the last sweep that weren't supposed to be there, which tells me they glove up."

"Who the hell would want to steal anything from me?" Sarah demands as she joins us. "I don't have much of anything, Hawk. Honestly, if they just asked me, I'd likely give them whatever they want. I don't have anything of value."

"Have you pissed someone off lately, Sarah?" Cullen asks as he walks out of the house and joins us.

"I don't think so. Why?"

He passes her a sheet of paper that's been placed in a clear evidence bag, and she reads aloud.

Bitch,

Where the hell are you? We need to talk. You have some explaining and apologizing to do, and I'm sick of waiting.

I'll be back.

"There's no signature. And it's typed, so no handwriting for me to obsesses over."

"That would have been too easy. Who's mad at you?" Hawk asks her.

"I don't—" But then she frowns and starts to shake her head slowly. "No way. That can't be it."

"It could be. Tell us," Cullen replies, and takes out a notebook to jot down notes.

As Sarah relays an incident between herself and a coworker named Angela, I feel myself get more and more pissed off. She didn't tell me about this, although she did say she had a run in with a coworker.

"I basically told her to kiss my ass, in way nicer words," she finishes. "And then I found out that the whole thing was a lie. She wanted to go to a concert. Her kid was at her mom's house."

"So, she wanted you to fill in for her, and you said no," Hawk summarizes. "That sounds pretty ordinary to me. It's not like you slept with her husband, or you have a kid bullying hers or anything."

"No, nothing like that. But she was *mad*. She's still not speaking to me, not that I really care. I needed the day off."

"Anyone else that has a grudge?" Cullen asks. "Exboyfriend, or maybe your ex-husband?"

"My one and only ex-boyfriend is right here," she says, pointing to me.

"No longer *ex*." I grin toothily.

"Trust me when I say," she continues, "my ex-husband gives absolutely *zero* shits about me. It's not the ex."

"Think it over," Hawk advises. "Good job on the security system, by the way. We'll take a look at the camera footage, just in case there's something to see."

"Yeah, well, if she was staying there, the asshole would have gotten to her, even *with* the alarm." My blood is fucking boiling. "The locks have been changed, and the security is tight. So, what, is this some kind of goddamn pro?"

Sarah swallows hard and slips her hand in mine.

"To be fair," Cullen says calmly, "the security is *good*, for a residence, but it's not fool-proof."

"Let me put it this way," I continue, frustration running through me. "If it was someone *you* loved, what would you do?"

Cullen and Hawk exchange a look, and then Cullen sighs. "I'd keep her with me, man. Move her in here, but make it look like she's still renting out there. I'd keep her close, and I wouldn't take chances. That's what I'd do if she were my girl or one of my sisters."

"The *girl* is standing right here," Sarah reminds us all. "A grown woman who can make her own decisions."

I look down at her, ready to argue, but she keeps talking.

"And I've decided that I'll move most of my stuff in here tomorrow morning."

All three of us grin at her.

"Good idea," Hawk says. "And not just because he's a man. There's safety in numbers. You notice they didn't try to break into the main house to see if you're in there."

"No," she agrees softly. "They didn't."

"I'm going to talk with my boss about the possibility of a little stakeout," Cullen says. "See if we can catch them in the act. In the meantime, stay alert. No alone time, unfortunately."

"That means no walking to work," Sarah adds.

"Absolutely not," I say before either of the officers can. "I'll drive you. Also, no walking the beach alone."

"What?" Sarah gasps, suddenly more horrified at that thought than a stranger in her house. "But, that's my *thing*."

"I'll walk with you," I offer, and when her shoulders droop, I rub circles on her back. "I'll even hang back a little and not bombard you with small talk so you can enjoy it without me harassing you."

"This is all a bunch of bullshit," she mutters, then turns to me. "Not you, of course. We can walk the beach together, but this is all ridiculous."

"Hopefully, we'll get it wrapped up quickly," Hawk says. "We'll be in touch."

Once they've driven away, Sarah and I walk into the kitchen, and I turn on the coffee maker. The sun will be up in an hour, so it's not worth going back to sleep.

Not that we could if we wanted to.

"I don't think it's Angela," Sarah says thoughtfully as she sits at the island and rests her chin in her hand. "I mean, she's mad at me, but she's not break-into-my-house mad."

"Maybe it *is* your ex."

Sarah scoffs and gratefully accepts the mug I offer her. "No. Definitely not. He likely doesn't even remember my name at this point. He couldn't wait to see the back of me, so I know he's not longing for any kind of apology. Besides, I have nothing to be sorry for. It's kind of the other way around there."

She sips her coffee thoughtfully.

"Was there anyone you were friends with in California that was mad at you?"

"I didn't have friends in California." She sets her cup on the counter and braces it between her hands. "I wasn't allowed to."

I narrow my eyes. "Allowed?"

"It was against his rules. No friends. No outside interests. I was at his beck and call."

"What about when he was gone?"

"Didn't matter." She shrugs a shoulder. "I did what he wanted, when he said. I didn't make my own decisions."

"Shit, Sarah. I'm sorry. I was trying to help with the art thing, but I acted just like him."

"No." She reaches over and covers my arm with her hand. "Absolutely *not*. You were acting out of love. He was a controlling ass. There's a huge difference."

"We're going to find who's doing this," I promise her.

"Huckleberry Bay isn't big. They can't hide for long. And when we do, I want just five minutes alone with them."

"You're sexy when you're acting all alpha and protective."

I don't smile in response.

"I'm serious, Sarah."

Chapter Eleven

Sarah

"Maybe I shouldn't go." I bite my lip and stare out the passenger side window as Tanner drives me from his house to Three Sisters Kitchen. "I don't want to get yelled at again."

"If Scott yells at you," Tanner says as he turns a corner, "you get up and leave. Simple as that. Did he say what he wants?"

"No." I twist my hands in my lap. "He just asked me if I'd meet him for lunch at Three Sisters. Our last conversation didn't end well."

"I say, see what he has on his mind. Just text me when you're finished, and I'll come get you."

"You know, this is stupid." I turn in the seat and face him as he parks by the curb. "It's been a *week,* and nothing's happened. Nothing at all, yet everyone thinks I need to be babysat. If I'm not with you, I'm at work or with one of the girls."

"You know it's the safest thing right now." He reaches over and drags his knuckles down my cheek, sending little currents of awareness down my body. "We're keeping you safe, sweetheart. You'll have your independence back soon."

Sighing, I nibble on my lower lip and then nod. "Okay. I'm stalling. I'll let you know about the ride."

I lean over and kiss him, then climb out of the car and walk inside the restaurant.

I *love* this place. The three women who own it, Cordelia, Mira, and Darla, are southern sisters who, I'm told, moved here several years ago and opened this beautiful, farm-to-table restaurant in the heart of Huckleberry Bay. The atmosphere is classy and is something Joanna Gaines would be proud of with that farmhouse-style décor that I salivate over.

The white walls, with glossy wood tables and little pops of green here and there from potted plants, make my heart sigh happily.

I am *so* excited that the sisters have gone into business with Luna, taking on the kitchen portion of the inn. I can't wait to see what they do with it.

"Hi there, Sarah," Cordelia says with that sweet southern accent. "How are you today, my darlin'?"

"I can't complain. How about you?"

"Oh, I'm just right as rain." She smiles with excitement. "Did you hear that we've started moving in appliances at the inn?"

"No, I hadn't heard. That's so exciting!"

"We are just beside ourselves. The next time you're

there painting, come on back, and we'll show you around if we're there. Of course, Mira's been there the most for this part of the process, as the kitchen is her baby. I swear, that girl has moonbeams in her eyes whenever she stares at that stove."

"She's going to make some delicious things on it." I grin at her. "And I can't wait to sample everything."

"She's come up with even *more* things since the last time we all got together. We'll have a girls' night and eat until we're bursting."

"Count me in."

"Oh, and Sarah, when you have time, I'd love to sit down with you and discuss the possibility of commissioning you to paint some pieces for the restaurant here. I just *love* what you're doing for the inn. I hope you don't mind that Luna gave me a sneak peek, but we could definitely use some local art for our walls."

I blink at her, surprised. "I'd like that."

"Great. Now, what can I do for you? I'm sure you didn't pop in just to have me talk your ear off."

"I always love chatting, but I'm meeting my brother, Scott, here."

"Oh, yes, he's here. Follow me."

She leads me through the dining room where Scott's sitting. Surprisingly, when I approach, my brother stands and pulls my chair out for me.

"Are you buttering me up for something?"

Scott shakes his head and sits across from me. "Thanks for meeting me here. I didn't know if you would after the way I spoke to you when you came to my place."

"I didn't know if I would, either," I reply and take a sip of ice water. "Did someone die, and now you have an opening on your friends list?"

He winces and leans his arms on the table. "I owe you an apology. For that, and for a lot of things. I just—"

He sighs and rubs his hand over the back of his neck.

"You really hurt me when you left, and I know I'm not a teenager anymore, but those feelings didn't just go away because you came home and said you were sorry."

I nod slowly. "I understand."

"But, I didn't have the right to snap at you like I did. That wasn't right, and I'm sorry for it."

"Thank you. Apology accepted."

His eyebrows climb in surprise. "Just like that?"

"Sure. Like you said, you were hurt. I wish it had been different. In my mind, it *would* have been different, and I have no one to blame for that but myself."

"Bullshit. You were married to a piece of garbage who controlled your every move. Luna and June have filled me in."

"I'm a grown woman," I counter. "I should have been stronger and stood up to him."

"Maybe," he says softly. "But I think it's more complicated than that."

"You're probably right."

My stomach has settled, my raw nerves are soothed, and I just want to reach out and hug my baby brother.

But I don't. Not yet.

"I heard that you've had some break-ins at your

house," he says after we've ordered lunch. "Any news on that?"

"No. There were no fingerprints, and the cameras didn't see their face. They were dressed in black, with a hoodie pulled low. Couldn't get a good look at them."

"Jesus, Sarah."

"I know. But, Tanner hasn't let me out of his sight unless I'm at work or with the girls, so I'm never alone. It's really annoying."

"You have to be careful," he says.

"Now you sound like Tanner."

"So, you're back with him, huh?"

"Yeah." I nod, watching him. His own shoulders have relaxed since I got here. He's so handsome, muscular, and tall. I bet the girls clamor for him. "You always liked Tanner, back in the day."

"Still do," he says. "He's a nice guy. He was stupid when he was young and broke it off with you, but most guys are stupid at that age."

"Even you?" I raise an eyebrow and watch as he laughs.

"Especially me."

"Are you seeing anyone?"

"Nah. I work crazy hours at the firehall. It's a tough job to have and maintain a good relationship. Unpredictable and dangerous."

"I think you speak from experience."

Our salads are set in front of us, and our water glasses refilled, and Scott continues.

"I've had a few girlfriends. I think chicks think the fireman thing is hot, no pun intended."

"Oh, yeah. I can vouch for that." I lick ranch dressing off my thumb. "Super hot."

"But in reality, it's being gone for days at a time, getting called in on your days off, and just generally not having a life of your own."

"You make it sound so glamorous."

He grins at me, and I can feel the shift in us. Things are going to smooth out and be fine. It might take some work, but I think I finally have my brother back.

"There's something else I have to tell you," he says, his face set in serious lines now. "And I don't know how you're going to take it."

"Am I an aunt?"

He smirks. "No. Mom died, Sarah."

I blink at him and drop my fork onto my plate. "What?"

"She died. I just got word yesterday. I guess it was a few weeks ago. They found her in her car, about a hundred miles away from where she'd been living."

"What happened?"

"Foul play, but I don't know what kind because they wouldn't tell me. It's an ongoing investigation."

"Where's Dad?"

"He wasn't with her. Authorities found him passed out in their camper, stoned and drunk. He claimed that he kicked her out months ago. Didn't care where she was or if she was dead."

"Jesus," I breathe and stare down at my salad. "What did they do with her remains?"

"Cremated her. They're sending her here, and I guess I'll bury her with her parents."

"June bought the property with the cemetery. No new internments."

Scott sits back at the news. "She bought a *cemetery*? Why in the hell would she do that?"

"It's attached to the church, and she's going to turn that into a house."

"Who would want their backyard to be a cemetery?"

"You'll have to ask her. The point is, I don't know if we can bury mom there. Maybe June will make an exception for us."

"She probably will," he murmurs. "I wasn't sad, Sarah."

My gaze returns to his. "What do you mean?"

"When I heard she was dead, I wasn't sad. I didn't feel much of *anything*."

"Why should we be sad? Sure, she gave birth to us, but she was *not* a mother to us in any way that counts. They barely kept a roof over our heads. Our friends' parents raised us, Scott. If they hadn't, we'd likely be just like them."

"I know it." He takes a bite of his salad. "I'll do the right thing and bury her, but I haven't heard from her since I was fourteen. That's longer than you were gone."

I cringe, and he shakes his head.

"I didn't say that to make you feel guilty. It's just the truth. Like, did she even remember that she *had* kids?"

"She didn't care. We were there to fetch them things and to make sure they didn't OD."

"You did most of that," he admits.

"Honestly, I'm surprised they're still alive. Well, you know what I mean. I figured they'd have passed a long time ago from the drugs and hard life they lived. I *knew* they were bad people from the time I was small. But when they walked away from this town, from you and me, and never looked back, I wrote them off."

"I know. No wonder we have abandonment issues."

"You're not wrong. I didn't help that."

"No, you didn't. But it also wasn't the same. You wanted to come back for me and couldn't. Mom and Dad didn't give a rat's ass."

"You won't take care of her alone, Scott. We'll figure out the burial together. I'll speak with June and let you know what I find out."

"I appreciate it. And for the record, I didn't ask you here today because of Mom. Yeah, I needed to tell you, but I wanted to see you so I could apologize."

"I'm glad you did." I smile over at him. "So, you're not dating *anyone*?"

He rolls his eyes and digs back into his salad. "You're not going to drop this, are you?"

"I *really* want to be an aunt."

"I NEED to bury someone in your cemetery," I inform June later that night when she and Luna walk into the inn where I've just finished painting.

"I've got a shovel," Luna offers. "And an alibi. Who did you kill?"

"See, you're a good friend," I reply, pointing at her. "That's *exactly* the response you should have in moments like this."

"But really, who did you kill?" June asks with a frown.

"*I* didn't kill anyone. My mom died."

They both gasp, and I jump, looking around the room. "What? Is there a spider? I saw a big one earlier. You're going to have to spray this place, Luna."

"Oh, honey, I'm so sorry," Luna says as she and June hurry to me and wrap me up in a big group hug.

"I'm fine," I assure them. "Really fine."

"How did you find out?" June asks.

"I had lunch with Scott today, and it went surprisingly well. He apologized for being an asshat."

"Good, he needed to," Luna says.

"He just found out about Mom yesterday. They found her in her car a few weeks ago."

I relay all the information I have, which isn't much.

"Like I told my brother, I thought they both would have passed away a long time ago." I turn to June. "Scott said he thought we'd bury her with her parents, but they're in the cemetery behind your new house."

"You can totally bury her there. I don't care."

"Don't I have to tell the city?" I ask. "File something

so there's a record?"

"Probably," Luna says, thinking it over. "I'm not sure. My ancestors are buried here on the property."

June and I turn to her in surprise. "What? You never told us that. I've never seen any graves."

"There's a piece of land that sits back in the trees," Luna says, pointing to the east. "They're in the trees."

"We seriously need to see that sometime," June adds. "I'm disgusted that we didn't know this sooner so we could scare the hell out of each other when we were kids."

"I didn't know until I stumbled upon it a few years ago. Asked my dad about it. I told him it was something I should know, since I'm the owner now."

"Why do I get the feeling that there are a lot of things your dad didn't tell you?" I ask.

"Because there were. I think he was just so excited to go with Mom somewhere warm to enjoy their retirement that he just forgot a bunch of stuff. So, I'm still learning as I go."

The door opens behind us, and in walks Tanner, along with Wolfe and Apollo.

"The three amigos," I say with a grin. "Hey, handsome."

"Hey yourself," Wolfe says with a wink, making us laugh.

"Ready to go home?" Tanner asks, searching my face. I told him about my mom when he picked me up from the restaurant, and I think he expects me to fall apart any second.

"Sure." I close the closet where I've been storing all of my supplies.

"What did you do to your hair?" Apollo asks June, a frown on his handsome face.

"I *cut* it, bonehead."

With that frown in place, he circles June, examining the new 'do. "I like it."

"Well, what a relief," she replies. "I didn't cut it for *you*."

But her cheeks have livened up at the compliment.

"I still like it." He tugs on a red strand as he walks past her toward the stairs. "I have to check something up here. See you guys later."

"See you," I call back with a wave and then turn back to Tanner. "I'm starving. Let's go home."

"Keep me posted on the burial," June says.

"We're here if you need us," Luna adds.

"I have *really* amazing friends." We've just pulled away from Luna's when I reach for Tanner's hand and give it a squeeze. "I'm seriously lucky."

"They're the best. All of them." He lifts my hand to his lips and nibbles. "I figured June would be cool with you putting your mom with her parents."

"Yeah, it's all good. I'll let Scott know tomorrow." I stretch my legs out and lean back in his comfy leather seat. "I have to get back to work tomorrow."

"What shift is it this time?"

"Breakfast," I reply and let my eyes fall closed as the car moves through town. I always fall asleep so easily in cars. "Seven to four tomorrow."

I feel the car come to a stop and open my eyes to find Tanner grinning at me.

"What?"

"Some things never change. You *always* fell asleep in the car."

"I know." I stretch and yawn. "But in my defense, I didn't sleep this time. I was just resting my eyes."

"If we had to go much further, you would have been snoring inside of two minutes."

"I don't snore." I narrow my eyes at him before getting out of the car and walking with him to the house. I haven't been in the little guest house since last week.

"It's a delicate, ladylike snore."

"I *purr*," I inform him as he unlocks the door. "There's a difference."

"Right. Okay." He laughs, and I walk straight back to the bedroom to change into something comfortable.

But right after I've pulled off my shirt and pants, Tanner appears behind me and glides his hands over my belly.

"Well, hello there."

His lips find the ball of my shoulder. "You're beautiful."

Tanner doesn't seem to ever get tired of telling me how much he wants me. And frankly, I don't get tired of hearing it.

"Did I interrupt?" His hands journey up to my breasts. My head falls back on his shoulder.

"I was just about to take off my bra."

I feel him smile against my skin, and then my bra falls to the floor at my feet.

"Thanks."

"Anytime." He nibbles a line up my shoulder to my neck. "I'm going to make love to you."

"Oh, good, I thought maybe you were just teasing me."

Suddenly, he pushes me forward, and sweet lust becomes primal arousal. "Press your hands on the wall."

I do, without hesitation. I widen my stance just a little, and Tanner's thumbs hitch in the sides of my underwear, then he peels them down my legs, and I step out of them.

I don't feel him stand back up behind me, and I look over my shoulder, only to find him squatted there, staring at my bare ass.

His hands work magic from my thighs, up over the globes of my backside, and then he presses his thumbs on either side of my lips and spreads me wide.

I cry out when he covers me with his mouth, and when his tongue laps at my lips, then inside of me, then down to my clit, I turn, but Tanner simply shakes his head.

"Face the fucking wall, Sarah, and back to where I put you."

I raise an eyebrow, but he's so damn sexy with my wetness on his lips and the fire in his eyes that I do what I'm told.

And I'm rewarded with a light smack on the ass and his mouth devouring me. I still cry out, but I don't move, careful to stay exactly where he wants me, even if I have to push up onto my toes and press harder into the wall.

It's a wonder that I don't break right through the drywall.

The first orgasm is a dam bursting. I can't help but push back against his face, and my God, it feels like my knees will buckle.

But they don't.

And after I've ridden that wave, he scoops me up and tosses me unceremoniously onto the bed and covers my body with his.

I reach for his cock, stroking it firmly from tip to root before he grits his teeth and sinks inside of me.

I expect this to be fast, maybe a little rough, but in true Tanner fashion, he surprises me and slows it down.

With his elbows planted in the bed on either side of my shoulders, he brushes my hair off of my cheeks and kisses the tip of my nose, then my lips so tenderly it brings tears to my eyes.

"You're incredible," he whispers.

"I love you," I whisper back, and feel him pause as he stares down at me in surprise. "I know I haven't said it back to you, but I don't want you to ever doubt that I *feel* it. It's just...scary to me."

"Not here." He shakes his head and pulls his hips back, then pushes in again in a long stroke that has my legs shaking. "Our love isn't scary, Sarah."

I cup his face as he kisses me, long and slow, and picks up the rhythm, pushing us both toward that beautiful edge, and then we fall over into oblivion together.

Later, when we've caught our breath, Tanner kisses my cheek gently.

"I'm hungry," I remind him, and I know that he's smiling into the darkness of the room. "I could eat my own cat at this point."

"I just ate your cat, and it was delicious."

The laugh erupts through me, and I push against him, rolling away. "You're so classy."

"No, I'm a man who gets to have sex on the regular with the hottest woman around. Also, you *are* delicious."

I just shake my head and pull on some clean pajamas, then stride out into the kitchen.

I planned to make dinner for him tonight. No, I'm not a fabulous cook, but there are a couple of staples that I can prepare.

"I hope you like mac 'n' cheese," I inform Tanner as he walks into the room. "We're having that and hotdogs."

He doesn't say anything at all, so I turn to look at him. "What?"

"Are we nine?"

"It's what I can cook," I reply and pull the blue box from the pantry. "You shouldn't have to cook every single day. I can do this. It's food."

"I'm not sure that's true," he replies as he pulls the box out of my hand before I can open it. "We're not eating that tonight."

I narrow my eyes at him and prop my hands on my hips. "Are you telling me that you're too *good* for this simple, inexpensive meal?"

"Yeah. I am."

"No, you're not." I take the box back. "I made this all the time for Scott and me, and I'm going to make it tonight, too."

"Is he coming over for dinner?"

"No, but that's a great idea." I pick up my phone to text my brother when Tanner just laughs and picks up Petunia off the floor.

Me: Hey! If you're hungry, come on over for dinner. I'm making our usual.

I set the phone down and grin at Tanner. "There. Sent it."

"Okay."

I eye him suspiciously. "You don't mind?"

"If you have dinner with your brother? Of course not. Do I mind that you're making pasta out of a box with plastic cheese? Absolutely."

"Don't be a baby."

My phone pings, and I check it.

"He's on his way over."

"This should be interesting, Petunia. You get to meet your uncle Scott."

"They've met." I set a pot of water on the stove to boil. "He came the night of the fire to make sure I was okay. But she was pretty upset, so she probably doesn't remember him."

Tanner just laughs and laughs, and finally, I throw a piece of hard pasta at his head.

"Stop laughing at me."

"You're the most adorable woman I've ever met in my life."

"I'm about to maim you."

That doesn't stop him from laughing, and then the doorbell rings.

"I'll get it," Tanner says.

I love bantering with him. I enjoy his sense of humor so much. I *know* that this meal doesn't thrill him. Tanner's an excellent cook, and this is definitely not something he'd make for himself.

But since I saw Scott earlier today, I've been craving it.

I hear the two men talking at the door, and when Scott walks into the kitchen, I grin over at him. "Hey."

"Thanks for the invite," he says and watches me dump the macaroni into boiling water. "You really *are* making that."

"Well, yeah. It's the only thing I know how to cook."

He smirks. "Seriously?"

"If you're going to mock me, you can leave."

But he just laughs and shakes his head. "Hey, it's food, and I'm hungry."

"*Is* it food, though?" Tanner asks.

"Don't you *dare* gang up on me," I warn them both, pointing the business end of my paring knife at them.

"What are you using that for?" Tanner wants to know.

"I have to cut up the hotdogs, of course."

He stares at me, then at Scott. "Are we going to die?"

"As long as you chew it, it's not a choking hazard," Scott says and pats Tanner on the back. "But I know the Heimlich, just in case."

AUGUST 19, 2002

DEAR DIARY,

I freaking hate my life so much. Mom stole all the money I had hidden. It was only $27, but it was mine, and she took it. Said I had to pay for rent.

Why was I born if this is what I have to live with?

TTYL,

Sarah

Chapter Twelve

Tanner

"**D**o whales have ears?"

I can't help but smile as I listen to the little boy talking his father's ear off as they walk around the gallery. He's full of questions.

"Yes, they even talk to each other," the dad replies.

"What? They can *talk*? I want to talk to a whale."

"They have a language we can't understand," is the father's reply.

"I'm gonna learn it." The boy's face is set in determined lines as he follows his dad to the next piece of art to examine.

It's early in the day, and these two are my first customers. Wayne won't be in for a while yet, and I usually take this time to answer emails, place orders, and balance my books.

But today, I just want to enjoy the art in my showroom and check out the deliveries that came in yesterday.

I took a lot of shit from my friends when I was a kid

whenever I said I wanted to work with art. I can't draw a stick figure to save my life, but I've always enjoyed studying paintings, sculptures, and just about any other art form out there.

At the sound of the bell above the door, I glance up and see the man with his boy walk out, and I begin my own journey through the space.

I have something for everyone. Cowboy bronzes, paintings of wildlife, and landscapes portraits.

It's an eclectic collection, but I've had success with it.

A lot of success, actually.

I straighten a canvas, then dust off a bronze piece of a woman holding a kitten, and I realize that this piece reminds me of Sarah and Petunia.

I don't have a place for it in my house right now, but if it doesn't sell soon, I'll consider it as a gift for Sarah.

With a half smile, I walk into the small storeroom next to my office. Wayne unboxed several new pieces yesterday afternoon, but we still have to catalogue them and get them ready for sale.

My phone rings in my pocket, and I'm surprised to see my aunt Becky's name on the display.

"Well, good morning, favorite aunt."

"You know, those words would mean so much more if I weren't your *only* aunt."

I laugh and remind myself that I need to get down to Newport to visit her. "How are you today?"

"Well, I'm doing fine, and I'd be better if this kitchen would ever get done."

"Are you *still* having issues with that?" I scowl at nothing in particular. "Do you want me to call someone?"

"No, they should be finished this week, thank all the gods above. Anyway, that's not why I was calling. Do you remember Ally Macky?"

"I don't think so."

"You know, she lived in that house on Cherry Lane that had the gargoyles on the eaves, like she lived in a damn castle or some such thing?"

"Oh, I remember the house, yeah. The new owner had the gargoyles removed."

"Good, they were awful. Anyway, do you remember her?"

"Not really. She was a *lot* older than me."

There's a slight pause. "She's *my* age."

I grin. "Exactly. A *lot* older than me."

"I'm going to pull on your ear the next time I see you for that."

I rub my free ear, already dreading it.

"What about her? Did she die or something?"

"Oh, goodness no. Why? Did somebody die? You never tell me the gossip."

"Focus, Aunt Becky."

"Right. Anyway, Ally told my friend, Eunice, who told my *other* friend, Franny, that you're living with Sarah Pedersen."

"Wait. *This* is why you asked if I remember Ally?"

"It's all for context," she insists and sniffs. "Is it true?"

"You can move out of Huckleberry Bay, but apparently, you can still get all the gossip."

"Not from *you*. Answer the question."

"Yeah. I'm living with her."

I explain to her how the situation came to be, and when I'm finished, she sighs in my ear.

"That's damn romantic."

Now I sigh in confusion. "It's *romantic* that someone broke into her house? Twice?"

"Obviously, you don't read the romance books, my boy. I'm assuming that she's not just sleeping on the couch."

"No. She's not. We're not going to get into *where* she's sleeping, Aunt Becky."

She laughs on the other end of the line now. "No, let's not. Bring her to see me, why don't you? Or, I'll come up there. I miss you, and I always had a soft spot for your girl."

"I know you did. We'll arrange it. Oh, and Aunt Becky, someone *did* die."

"What? Who?"

I tell her the little I know about Sarah's mom.

"They were horrible people," Becky says softly. "I don't like to say that about anyone, because there's always *some* good in someone, but those two were just *horrible*. I felt for those kids, and I'm relieved that they both turned into good people, despite the shit they came from."

My eyebrows climb in surprise. Aunt Becky *never* swears.

"They're both doing great," I assure her. "Now, what other pieces of gossip do you have?"

"None to share," she says. "Watch your back, Tanner.

I know you want to protect Sarah, but I need you to be careful, too. I don't think I'd ever recover if something happened to you."

"I'll be careful," I assure her, just as the bell over the door jingles. "I have to go. I have customers."

"Alright, then. Have a good day, honey."

"You, too."

I stop short when I walk out to the showroom and see Sarah stomping back and forth.

"What's wrong?"

"First, don't yell at me. Yeah, I walked here alone, but it's literally like two blocks, and I'm just so pissed off that I had to get the hell out of there on my break."

I nod slowly, watching as she breathes hard and grinds her teeth together in absolute *rage*.

"Wanna talk about it, pretty girl?"

"I want to fucking *punch something*."

I cross my arms over my chest and let her pace and work off some aggression. I've never seen her this angry, and it's spectacular and a little frightening, all at once.

"Who pissed you off?"

Her eyes narrow on me, and I worry that I should have waited to speak to her, but then she blows out a breath and seems to sag as she lets just a little of the rage go.

"Angela is a stone-cold *bitch*."

"This is the one who lied to you about why she needed her shift covered last week?"

"Yeah. Listen, I don't give two fucks if she doesn't want to talk to me. I don't *care*."

"Don't blame you."

"But apparently, me giving her *no* reaction has pissed her off all over again, and now she's stealing my tips."

I straighten, the rage she let go now filling my chest. "Excuse me?"

"All of my cash tips. I've had sixteen tables already this morning, which is a shit ton. Looks like tourist season is starting early. Anyway, only five of those put their tips on their credit cards. The rest were cash."

"And she's swooping by to snatch it up before you get the chance?" I guess, and she nods emphatically.

"I caught her. But when I called her out on it, she just shrugged and said, '*Well, I guess if you were a better server, people would tip you.*'"

"Oh, fuck that."

"Right?" She jabs her finger into the air, pointing at me. "*Right?* I'm so mad. I bet she's copped more than fifty bucks from me."

"You need to talk to someone *right now*, Sarah. Not me, but Gordy or Sunny."

"Oh, I plan to. I just knew that if I did in that moment, I would make a scene and probably get fired."

"Make the fucking scene." I stalk over to her and take her hands in mine. "For once, just make the goddamn scene, Sarah. Throw the biggest fit that Angela has ever seen, and make it *crystal* clear that she's not to fuck with you ever again."

"I'm going to," she decides and grabs my face on both sides, yanks me to her for a hard kiss, and then pushes away. "I'm going to right now."

She stomps away, and knowing that I can't miss this, I march right behind her, locking the gallery door on the way.

Her stride is hard and purposeful, and if I were Angela, I'd be damn scared right now.

"She thinks she can fucking *steal* from me?" Sarah rants, her voice shaking with anger. "I won't have it. I will *not* have it."

Make that terrified. I'd be terrified if I were Angela, and I make a mental note to *never* piss her off like this.

It's a wrath no man has any business evoking from a woman. Not if he values his neck, anyway.

Sarah yanks the door of the diner open, and I have to move fast to catch it so it doesn't slam in my face.

"You," Sarah says loudly, pointing at Angela. "In the back, now."

"I have customers," Angela begins, but Sarah snarls at her.

"I said *now*."

Sunny and I share a look, then follow the other two back to the break room.

"What's happening?" Sunny whispers to me.

"Angela's been stealing Sarah's tips all morning."

"Oh, hell no." Sunny makes a move to walk over and take care of things, but I put my hand on her shoulder, stopping her.

"Let Sarah fight this battle."

"You've been swiping cash off of my tables all goddamn morning," Sarah begins, shooting daggers at her foe. "You can hate me all day long, but you won't fucking steal from me, Angela."

"I don't know what you're talking about." She examines her chipped nails, as if she's not worried in the least about what Sarah has to say, although her eyes do slide over to see that Sunny and I are listening. "People just don't tip piss-poor waitresses. You should step up your game."

"Uh-oh," I mutter when Sarah's already heaving chest quickens. "You might want to call the cops. I have bail money."

Sunny just shakes her head.

"I'm going to file charges," Sarah says, her voice much calmer than her body language. "I'm filing charges for the stolen tips, and for you breaking into my house."

Angela's jaw drops. "Wait, what? I didn't break into your stupid house. You don't have anything that I want."

"Obviously I do, because you've stolen it from me. And now that I think about it, my tips were low the other day, too. I think you've been skimming off my tables ever since I wouldn't cover your shift just so you could go to a motherfucking *concert*. And you're going to pay for it."

"I didn't break into your house, you stupid bitch," Angela yells back. "But yeah, I took your money. It'll teach you a fucking lesson not to be a cunt to your coworkers."

"And that's all I need," Sunny says brightly. "Angela, collect your things and get out of here."

"No way," Angela counters, shaking her head wildly. "I'm not getting fired over that sack of trailer-trash garbage. She's lying about all of it. She's just like her mother, probably hiding the money so she can make me give her more for drugs. That's what those people do."

Now, the woman sounds like a lunatic and is changing the story again.

"That's enough," Sunny snaps, but Sarah's already flown into action, her fist reared back, and I snag her around the waist and hang on with all my might, preventing her from clocking Angela in the nose.

"Let me at her," Sarah snarls, but I hold on tight.

"She's not worth it," I say into her ear. "She's already lost her job. Don't you lose yours, too."

"I don't care about the job."

But I know that she does, and we watch together as Angela rants and yells, but she gathers the stuff out of her locker and turns to Sarah.

"You're going to pay for this, you piece of shit."

"Oh, good, more threats. I'll add it to the complaint I'm going to file today."

Before Angela can rage anymore, the cops show up, two younger guys that I don't know by name, and they escort Angela out the front door.

Sarah's shaking now, still breathing hard, when Sunny approaches her.

"I assume Gordy called the cops," she says and lays her hand on Sarah's shoulder. "I'm pretty sure the whole restaurant heard that fun exchange. Shake it off, honey. She's not worth this. You go home and gather yourself. I'll call in Willow. She'll cover once I tell her what happened."

"No," Sarah says, and takes a deep breath, settling herself. "I'm okay. I can finish the shift. Unless you're firing me."

"I should," Sunny says. "You didn't handle that in the best way. You should have come to me, and then we would have figured things out. But that woman has been antagonizing you for a while now, and I suspect I would have lost it, too. Now, let's get back to work. I'm pretty sure the people out there are pissed off by now."

She walks away, and Sarah just turns and *thuds* right into my arms.

"Hey." I squeeze her tight and kiss the top of her head. "You can do this, babe. Call me if you need me."

"Thanks. I'll need wine later. Maybe tequila."

"We can do that."

She squares her shoulders and goes back to work, heading for the kitchen to pick up orders.

I hear her apologize to Gordy, who just shakes his head and mumbles something about dramatic women, but he winks at her, and she smiles back at him gratefully.

It seems the storm has passed.

"I BROUGHT ice cream and root beer," June announces as she walks into my house, holding the bag in the air. "Sarah loves a root beer float."

"Who doesn't?" I ask and take the bag from her. "Thanks. We'll add this to the cupcakes. You'll all pass out from a sugar coma."

"Nah, we can handle it," Luna replies as Wolfe gently rubs circles on her back. "Do you have tongs for the cheese?"

"There are special cheese tongs?" I ask. "Can't we just use our fingers?"

"Savages," June mutters, and Apollo walks through the door. "Oh, look, the king of the savages has arrived."

"Thanks for noticing." He smiles and saunters over with a bag of his own. "I brought the tequila. I also have chips and salsa."

When I called everyone after returning to the gallery, we decided that we needed to have dinner tonight, with all of Sarah's favorite things, to help her work off the rest of her anger.

"Sunny should be dropping off Sarah any minute," I inform them, but the back door is already opening, and in walks Sarah.

"Is everyone here?" she calls out. "There are a million cars in the driveway."

She stops short when she sees us all gathered in the kitchen, and her pretty eyes fill with tears.

"Uh-oh," Apollo mutters. "She's gonna blow."

"We thought you could use some tacos," Luna says and crosses to Sarah to give her a hug. "Everyone needs tacos after a shitty day of laying the smackdown at work."

"Let's not forget the tequila," Apollo adds, holding up the bottle.

June rolls her eyes, but Sarah gives him a watery laugh. "Thanks, guys. This is definitely what I need. But first, a quick shower to get the grime of the day off of me.

Including the hex I'm sure Angela threw my way on her way out the door."

"Let's go." I hold my hand out for hers.

"No sex while I'm in the house," June calls after us, making Sarah laugh. "Absolutely *none*."

"I can't promise anything," I call back. When we're alone, I hug her to me. "How you doing?"

"Ugh, I'm tired. But the day was fine. The rest of it, anyway. Let me take this shower, and I'll be out to join everyone."

"Is it okay that I did this? Invited everyone over?"

"It's more than okay. I didn't know that I needed it until I saw everyone. It's nice to feel supported and loved, you know?"

"Yeah. I know." I lean in and press my lips to hers. "Get comfy. The food's ready when you are."

"Oh, get started. Don't make them wait for tacos."

She saunters into the bathroom, and I return to the others.

"She says to go ahead and eat, and she'll catch up when she's done in there," I inform them.

"Don't have to tell me twice," Wolfe says as he grabs a plate. "Hey, is anyone in the market for a car?"

"You're *selling* cars now?" I ask him.

"Just this one. Someone dropped it off to be fixed three months ago. Been fixed for almost that long, but they haven't come back to get it, or pay for it, nor have they responded to my calls or letters. So, I'll sell it."

"You can do that?" June asks. "You don't have the title."

"It's abandoned property," Apollo adds. "It's likely on the form you sign when you leave your truck for an oil change, or something, that if you don't come back to claim it within a certain amount of time, then you're forfeiting the property."

"Interesting," June muses and pops a chip into her mouth. "Does that happen very often?"

"Thankfully, no," Wolfe says. "I don't have time to sell cars. It's a pain in the ass, but I have to recoup the costs of fixing it."

"What was wrong with it?" Apollo asks.

"Rear axle was shot and needed brakes and a general tune-up. But it's good to go now."

"I feel human again."

Sarah walks into the room, and everyone gets quiet and stares at her, including me.

"I did get dressed, right?" She looks down at her T-shirt and jeans and then frowns at us. "Why is everyone staring at me?"

"So, are you in the market for a car, Sarah?" Wolfe asks her.

"Yeah, right," she scoffs and makes a beeline for the taco buffet on my countertop. "I mean, I guess I *could* afford a car payment, but I really don't want to. Huckleberry Bay is small enough to walk almost everywhere, and if I need to go to the inn, I can hitch a ride."

She shrugs, and I share a look with Wolfe.

"How much are you asking, Wolfe?"

"Wait, *you* have a car for sale?" Sarah laughs and

adds sour cream to her taco. "I definitely can't afford your Ferrari, but thanks for the vote of confidence."

"It's a Honda," he replies. "SUV. It's not new by any means, but it runs great now that Zeke and I have had our hands in it."

Her eyes narrow, and I can see the wheels turning.

"It was a car that someone dropped off for repair," I explain to her. "They never came back to get it, and he just wants to get paid for the job and get the car off his property."

"Basically," Wolfe agrees. "Let's talk about it. It would be a good car for you. I should have thought about it before."

"I'll have a look," she says with a nod, her mouth full of food. "Look at me, adulting like a rock star."

"So, I have to know," Apollo says. "Did you knock the bitch on her ass? I don't have many details."

"I tried." Sarah scowls at me. "But this one held me back and wouldn't let me. I would have really cleaned her clock."

"You prevented a girl fight?" Apollo demands, clearly disgusted.

"I prevented Sarah from an assault charge," I counter.

"Ah, well, there is that," Apollo replies.

"I don't even remember Angela from when we were kids," Sarah says with a frown. "Do you guys? She said she knew who my parents were, and that I come from trash, which isn't wrong, but I don't remember her."

"She's younger than us," June replies. "By quite a bit,

I think. But she might be about Scott's age. Mid-twenties."

"That makes sense," Sarah says. "I wouldn't have known her, then. Man, she hates me."

"Well, to be fair," Luna says, and winces, "she had it bad for Scott, from what I hear. Like, *bad.* And I think they dated a little, but he ended up breaking it off for some reason or another."

"She must have gotten over it, because she had a baby with someone else. I think she was married."

"Still, he scorned her, and you're Scott's sister, so it doesn't surprise me that she wasn't nice to you," Luna says.

"The weird thing is, we got along just fine for a long time. Then, a few weeks ago, she decided to get all psycho on me." Sarah shrugs. "Oh well, who knows what makes people tick? Not me. I need a margarita."

"Coming up." I assume the role of bartender and slice a lime in half. "Who's in?"

Chapter Thirteen

Sarah

I have a new car. Well, new to *me*, anyway, courtesy of a couple grand and a good friend named Wolfe. I tried to pay him fair market value, but he wouldn't have it.

I've just left his fancy garage, the one on his personal property near Luna's lighthouse. He's working out of there until the garage in town is rebuilt.

I'm driving through Huckleberry Bay with the windows down and the music turned up.

When I pull into Tanner's driveway, I'm surprised to see a van sitting there. I didn't think we were expecting company.

Tanner himself pokes his head out of the side of the big white van and grins at me as I park to the side.

"Hey, I like your new ride."

"Thanks." I bounce over to him and kiss him square on the mouth, then turn to admire the red Honda with him. "It runs great, of course, and, well, it's the first car

I've owned since I was nineteen, so it's kind of the best vehicle with four tires."

"Agreed." He wraps his arms around me from behind and squeezes me tightly against him. "And when we get back, we'll go for a long ride in it."

I look over my shoulder and up at him with a frown. "Where are we going?"

"Well, I don't know if you noticed this rather large van parked behind us."

"I did. Who's here? I didn't expect company."

"No one's here." He kisses my nose, and I turn to face him. "I rented it. It's a luxury travel van, and we, my love, are going camping."

"We're going *camping*." I blink, and then I squeal and launch myself up at him. "I want to see the inside."

"Your castle awaits." He gestures for me to climb in ahead of him, and when I get on the first step, I gasp.

"Holy shit, Tanner. This isn't camping. This is *glamping*. There's a freaking chandelier in here. And a full bathroom."

The inside is done in a farmhouse style and reminds me of Three Sisters Kitchen. There's shiplap and subway tile, butcher block countertops in the tiny kitchen, and hardwood laminate on the floor.

It's *fancy*.

"Just wait until you see where we're going. You and Petunia will get a kick out of it."

I spin around and stare at him, stunned. "We get to take my cat?"

He frowns, then opens a little compartment that has a cat-sized hole in the front and reveals a litter box.

"We'll put her in her harness and leash," he says reasonably.

"I love you." I yank him to me and kiss the hell out of him. "Like, a lot. More than a lot."

He laughs and tucks my hair behind my ear. "I love you, too. I even love the cat. Now, let's get packed up so we can hit the road."

"Are we going far? I have to work tomorrow."

"No, you don't." His eyes are soft and sweet as he looks over at me. "I've arranged for the week off, paid. You need a break. *We* need a break. So, this will be home for the next five days, just you and me...and the cat."

I would cry, but I have too much to do to give into the happy tears. I've *never* been camping, and I've always wanted to go.

I love being in the woods with the trees and the wildlife.

"Then let's get a move on and get the hell out of here."

I run ahead of him and into the house, where we pack up the groceries that Tanner already bought. Once those are put away and organized in the van, I run back into the house to pack some clothes and necessities and all of Petunia's things. The last thing to go out is the feline herself, who doesn't seem to be super excited about it, until we're in the van, and she finds a little perch up by the window to watch the world go by as we drive.

The coastline is rugged, jagged even, and never ceases to take my breath away.

Tanner heads south, taking his time on the windy Highway 101.

"How far are we going?" I ask him.

"A few hours," he replies. "Just southern Oregon. And that's all I'm going to tell you."

"Okay." I settle back into the seat and feel my eyes get heavy.

"Go to sleep," he urges.

And that's the last thing I hear before drifting off.

"Hi there, we're checking in. Last name is Hilleman."

"Ah yes, here you are." I open my eyes and see that we've pulled up to a one-man kiosk, and a young gentleman in a brown jacket is typing on a tablet. "You're in slot seventy-one, and everything is set up for you. Do you need help connecting to the electric and water?"

"I don't think so, but I'll let you know if I screw anything up," Tanner replies and signs a sheet of paper, then passes it back to the man.

"Just drive straight ahead and follow the signs. Have a great week, and welcome."

He hands Tanner a few brochures and then nods, and we're off.

"I love the trees." I roll down the window and lean out so I can take a deep breath. "Smells so clean. I know we have the same thing in Huckleberry Bay, but this just hits different."

Within minutes, we've reached our site.

"Close your eyes," Tanner instructs me. "Just for a few minutes."

I comply. It's a good thing I don't get carsick because he has to whip the van around, forward and backward, I assume, to get it just the way he wants it.

"Keep them closed."

I hear him hop out of the van and move stuff about. And just when I think I might fall asleep again, he opens my door and brushes his knuckles over my cheek.

"Okay, open your eyes, pretty girl."

I do, and in front of me is simply woods. No other RVs are parked in the slots; it's just the two of us.

"Come on."

Tanner takes my hand and leads me around to the back of the van, and that's when my breath catches. All I can do is stare.

We're parked near the edge of a cliff, maybe a hundred feet back, and through the trees on either side of the camping space is a view unlike any other I've ever seen.

Big, brown rocks jut up out of the sand, almost as tall as this cliff, and the waves crash around them, sending sprays of water into the air. Birds fly around them. They obviously have nests high up, out of reach of the tide waters.

The trees are so vividly *green* against that blue water with frothy white waves and the bluest sky in the world.

"Wow," is all I can say. "This could be the best view on the planet."

"I'm inclined to agree." His hand's still in mine, and he squeezes. "Come see this."

The doors on the back of the van are open. The bed looks out to *this* view, and there are lights strung over to the trees, above a fire pit where we can cook.

Well, *he* can cook, and I'll roast marshmallows.

Petunia's already in her harness, and her leash is tied to the inside of the van, where she's lying on the bed, enjoying the view of the water, as always.

"Can we just live here all the time?"

He laughs and pulls something out from under the bed.

"Hold that thought," he says, and before my very eyes hangs a hammock between two trees.

"I call that spot," I inform him. "I'm going to read and sleep there all the livelong day, while I listen to the ocean."

"It's all yours." He pulls me to him and kisses me softly in that way he does that turns my knees to jelly and my heart to mush. "Are you happy?"

"So happy. I already feel lighter."

"Excellent. Now, let's get cozy. Do you need a snack?"

"Uh, this is vacation. Of *course,* I need a snack."

"That's the third marshmallow I've lost to the fire." I stick my bottom lip out in a pout.

"You leave it in the flame too long," Tanner says. "Just get a little sizzle going, then pull it out."

"That's what she said." I snort out a laugh when he narrows his eyes at me. "Come on, that was funny. I like mine *burnt*. Like, black. Give me all the charcoal on this sucker."

"It's going to fall off," he warns me as I impale another marshmallow. He's eaten three s'mores already, and I haven't had even one.

Because I'm trying to get the marshmallow just perfect. This time, when it starts to sizzle, I count to three, then pull it out and let it burn outside of the fire. And when it just starts to turn black, I blow it out.

"Success," I announce with glee. "Finally. I'm starving."

"You just ate a burger and a hobo packet."

"I'm starving for sugar," I clarify, and build my little s'more sandwich, then take a bite. "Oh, my gah, so good."

Tanner reaches over and rubs some chocolate off my lip, then sucks it off his own thumb.

We can't see the water anymore in the dark, but the sky is scattered with millions of stars, and I can even see the Milky Way.

"It's incredible out here." Tanner and I huddle up with a blanket wrapped around us and settle back in the double camping chair that he brought along to look up at the sky.

"I should have thought to bring a telescope," he says

softly. "With no light noise out here, I bet you can see some awesome things."

"We could probably even do that at home." I lean my head on his shoulder. "Do you see the Milky Way?"

"No, where?"

"There." I point due west. "You have to really hunt without a time-lapse camera, but you can make it out."

"Holy shit, I see it."

We sit in silence for a while, just listening to the sounds of the forest around us, the waves below, and the fire crackling as it dies down.

"I've always wanted to camp," I whisper. "To just be in the quiet. In the stillness."

"Why didn't you go?" he asks.

"Life gets busy." I shrug and bite my lip. "Anthony said a hotel without room service was camping, and he'd be damned if he'd do it. So, we didn't. But it's okay, because even if he had done it just to humor me, it would have sucked. This is *so* much better. I'm glad I got to go with you."

"I think we should make this a yearly thing." He kisses my temple. "Once a year, we take a week to unplug like this."

"Hey, I'm always down. Where did you rent the van? I haven't seen anything like it anywhere near Huckleberry Bay."

"Portland has a few places that rent them out," he replies. "I called around until I found the one I wanted, and they delivered it to the house."

"Wow, they *delivered* it? Fancy."

He smirks and pokes at the fire, sending sparks in the air and the logs to glowing.

"I didn't want to waste time driving up to Portland to get it. We only have a week."

"I mean, a week is plenty of time, even if we had to go fetch the van."

He turns his eyes to mine. "I have a feeling that by the time the week is up, it won't feel like enough time at all."

"You're probably right." The night air cools quickly, and I feel a chill run through me, making me shiver. "I haven't thought about the diner even once all day. I think that's a record for me."

"There's no need to," he says. "I see you brought some paint supplies with you."

"Oh, yeah. And I'm especially glad that I did, now that I know what our view is. I already have a couple of projects in mind. What will you do for a whole week with nothing on your agenda? Won't you be bored?"

"No." He leans back again and draws me close. "I won't be bored. I plan to do some hiking, reading, cooking... And I'm going to make love to you pretty much all the time."

"Wow, that's quite a list of fun activities."

He laughs, and then his hand drifts down my arm and over to cover my breast.

"I think you're going to enjoy them."

"Do I have to hike with you?"

"Absolutely not." He shakes his head. "We can do

some things alone. I think that's part of the fun of camping."

"Me, too." I sigh happily. "Yeah, this is definitely a new tradition."

A BIRD SQUAWKS OVERHEAD, startling me, and I accidentally push my brush over the canvas, ruining the work I just spent an hour doing.

"Well, shit," I mutter, staring at the long green streak. "Hmm, maybe I could turn it into a fallen tree. Or a meadow, instead of the water view."

I narrow my eyes, giving it thought, and decide to go with the meadow. I didn't bring a lot of materials with me, so to waste this canvas isn't really an option for me.

"Maybe Luna could use it in the inn," I mutter as I switch gears and reach for different paint colors. "It'll find a home."

"Hello, neighbor!"

I frown and look around. There haven't been any other campers near us in two days, and it's been so nice to be alone.

Hell, we had sex with the doors open on the van last night. Now, that was hot.

I walk around the van and see a very pregnant woman making her way to me. She's in jeans and an oversized blue top that covers her belly. She looks to be in her early twenties, barely out of college.

"Uh, hi," I reply and force a smile on my face. "Can I help you?"

"Oh, no, I'm fine. I just wanted to come say hello. I'm just up the road, in my little pull trailer. It sure is pretty out here, isn't it?"

"Yeah, it is. Is your husband setting up your site?"

"What's that?" Her eyebrows climb, and then she shakes her head. "No. No husband. Just me and this little one."

"I know it's none of my business, but...you're *very* pregnant."

"I am," she says with a laugh and rubs her belly. "Like, so, *so* knocked up."

"Should you be camping by yourself when you're that far along?"

"Eh, it's okay. I mean, yeah, the doctor told me that it's probably not a great idea, but I'll be fine. I just really wanted to get out of the city, you know?"

"Where are you from?" Panic is starting to settle into my stomach. What if she goes into labor? What if she has the baby in the *woods*?

"California," she replies. "Not too far away."

"So, northern California, then."

"Sure." Her smile is bright, and I can't help but wonder if something is just...off.

"Are you all right?" My words are careful. "Do you need help with anything?"

"Nope. I'm great. I just wanted to pop over and say hi so I don't startle you if I start a fire and stuff. We're pretty isolated up here."

"Exactly," I mutter to myself as she waddles away, back the way she came. "At least I know if we hear screams in the night, it's likely to be her delivering a baby."

I watch her disappear around a corner, and then I return to my easel. I've just put the finishing touches on the new painting when Tanner returns from a hike, looking all sweaty and sexy in his dark blue T-shirt and cargo shorts. His backpack hangs on his shoulders, and he's even wearing a hat.

He looks so *outdoorsy*.

"Hi, adventurer." I smile at him as he approaches and kisses me without touching me. "How was your hike?"

"Dirty," he says, a little out of breath. "I wasn't expecting so much mud. So it was a slick hike, and I need a damn shower."

"Well, luckily for you, we have one. You do that, and I'll make us some sandwiches for lunch."

"Deal."

He disappears into the van, and I can hear him moving around as I wash my hands and get to work making lunch.

It's been like this since we arrived. We each spend a portion of the day doing whatever we want to. He hikes, and I paint. Or he reads, and I nap. We don't have to be in each other's back pocket to enjoy each other, and I really love that. I especially love that we're safe here, and that we can spend some time apart without me needing someone else to babysit me.

We can just relax. That hasn't happened in several

weeks, and I didn't realize how much I needed it until we got here.

Then, we eat something and spend the afternoon together. Today, I'm hoping we can find the beach access and do some exploring at low tide. I've heard there are a ton of agates and geodes to find down this way, and I want to go hunting for them.

When Tanner steps out of the van *naked*, I feel my eyes go wide, and I hurry over to him.

"You can't be naked."

"I'm going to get dressed. I just thought I'd air dry first. Besides, you said you like it when I'm naked."

"I do." I laugh and push him back toward the van. "But we have a neighbor, and I'm quite sure you don't want to flash her."

I fill him in on my visitor as he dresses in clean clothes.

"Wait. There's a possibility that she could have a baby here?"

"Well, I don't know exactly how far along she is," I admit. "But she's *very* pregnant, Tanner. Like, big. So I assume she's getting close to her due date."

"Great. I have no idea how to deliver a baby."

I glance over when he gets quiet and shake my head. "Don't look at me. I don't know how either."

"But you're a woman. You have natural instincts."

"That's not the same as medical training." My voice is dry as I pass him his plate. "I've never seen a baby being born."

"I wonder why she came up here by herself." He

takes a bite and then sighs. "God, that's good. I'm starving."

"How far did you hike?"

"About six miles. Felt like it was uphill both ways."

"I love you, but I don't ever want to do that with you."

He takes another bite. "That's okay. I don't do it often. Your painting is beautiful, by the way."

"It was a mistake. Bird scared the hell out of me, and I smeared green paint, so it evolved from a seascape to a meadow. It's not bad."

"It's excellent. I work in art. I know these things."

"Thanks. I guess, if you wanted to ask that customer you told me about, I could sell it to her if she's interested."

He stops chewing, and his eyes fly to mine in surprise. "Really?"

"Sure." I shrug, looking over at the painting. "I don't think it'll fit at the inn, and I don't have a place for it. If she wants it, she can buy it. And if not, I'll gift it to someone."

"I'll take a photo of it and send it to her, see what she thinks. If you're sure."

I nod and bite my sandwich. "I'm sure. The past couple of weeks have taught me that although I love Gordy and Sunny and the diner—I don't even hate the actual job all that much, although waiting tables is damn hard work—I just don't want to do it forever. It's fine for now. In fact, it's great for now. But it's not my forever job."

We're quiet as we eat, and then I can't help but keep talking.

"Remember that day I met with Scott at Three Sisters?"

"Sure."

"Cordelia said that she'd like to speak with me about doing some work for them. Between commissioned work and anything that I might sell through you, or maybe even online, I think I can make at least what I'm making at the diner."

"It's likely that you'll end up making more, Sarah."

"I don't need more, although that would be nice." I shrug and finish my sandwich. "I have everything that I need with what I have. If I can make my living from the art, I'd be stupid to pass that up."

"I'm happy that you made this decision. And there really is no pressure."

"As long as I can keep painting, there's no pressure." I grin at him and reach for a bag of marshmallows, popping one into my mouth. "Wanna find a way down to the beach and search for some shiny things?"

"Doesn't everyone?" His lips twitch and then open wide when I toss him a marshmallow, and he actually catches it. "Thanks."

"Let's lock everything up and go down for a while."

"Lock up?" He raises an eyebrow. "That means Petunia doesn't get any fresh air."

"We're in the shade, and it's not hot. Besides, I don't have a great feeling about the girl down the road. There's just something...off about her."

"Okay, we'll lock up when we leave, then."

He stands and offers me a hand to help me to my feet.

"Maybe she won't be here long." I slide on my hiking shoes and grab my gathering bag for my treasures.

We don't have to go far to find a path that gets us down to the sand below. It's going to be a bitch to climb back up, but we'll deal with that when we get there.

"This is the *perfect* inlet for geodes and stones," I inform Tanner. "There's some sand, but it's also very rocky. Obviously, the tide brings in all kinds of stuff."

We make our way over rocks and tide pools, stopping here and there to examine the sea life on the rocks.

"I've never seen a purple starfish." I point to the little guy clinging to a boulder. "Not *that* purple. Wow."

"And look at this crab," Tanner says. "His shell is insane."

We keep moving. I just *know* that I'm going to find something amazing down here.

And then I spot it.

"Right here," I say in excitement as I pick my way over slick rocks to the oddly shaped one, right in the middle. "This is a crystal geode."

"How can you tell?"

"The shape. It's heavy, too. Oh, and listen."

I shake it next to his ear and watch as he blinks in confusion.

"There's water in this one. Water that's probably been trapped in there for thousands of years."

"And you're going to set it free?"

"Hell yes, I am. I can't wait to see what's inside."

I stash it in my bag.

"You should have been a geologist," Tanner says as

we pick our way over the rocks, careful not to slip and fall.

It's slick down here.

"This is a *big* agate," I announce as I lift the gorgeous orange rock in my hand. "So pretty."

"I think this could be something." He holds a rock out to me, and I squeal with excitement.

"Another geode! This one is smaller, but that's what it is. Good job, babe."

"I'm a quick study."

We discover a couple of small things here and there, and then I stretch my back, a little sore from bending over for so long.

"I think this is plenty. I don't want to take too much."

"I can't wait for you to crack those open," he says as he takes my hand to make sure I make it back to the sand safely. "How do you do it?"

"With a chisel and hammer."

"We don't have those things here." He purses his lips in thought. "Looks like we're making a trip into town."

MARCH 6, 2005

DEAR DIARY,

Luna's mom got me a whole set of paints with canvases and an easel for my birthday! I couldn't believe it! I've never seen anything more beautiful. I painted two pictures and took one to Luna and one to June as a thank you for everything that they do for me. They immediately hung them in their rooms and were so excited to get them.

It made me really happy.

I can't wait to paint more.

TTYL,

Sarah

Chapter Fourteen

Tanner

"These will do," she says, pointing to the cheapest chisel and hammer the hardware store has.

"You'll break them on those rocks." I shake my head and grab the more expensive ones, then smile when Sarah's brows bunch together in a scowl. "This way, you'll have these for all the geodes you find in the future."

"Well, that's true. I'll make a little toolbox for our glamping trips."

We add a small, red toolbox to our pile of purchases that also includes a towel to throw away and a bucket, then make our way to the checkout counter.

"I'm *starving*," Sarah says when we leave the store.

"It's been a little while since the sandwiches," I agree. "Should we take a pizza back with us?"

"You get me," she decides as she fastens her seatbelt. "I like that about you."

I put our order in at a local pizza spot online, and

while we wait for it to be ready, Sarah grabs her phone to take some photos of the cute little town but frowns when she looks down at the screen.

"It says I don't have any service."

I check my own phone and shake my head. "I have one bar. Maybe power off and back on again."

"It sucks when we move in and out of coverage so much. Confuses the phone."

She powers off the phone, then waits a couple of minutes and turns it back on. "Nope. No service."

"That's odd."

My own phone pings with a message that our order is ready, so I walk inside to collect the food, and when I come back out, Sarah's taking some photos.

"The camera still works," she says with a shrug. "I'll figure the rest out when we get home in a couple of days. I don't really need it, and we have yours for emergencies."

"Good idea." With Petunia sunning herself on the dash, I start the van, and we head back to our home away from home.

"Was it this bumpy going in?" Sarah wants to know as we bump along the road that leads into the campground.

"Yes. You were just asleep."

"That's right."

I check in with the kiosk, and before long, we're back at our spot. And, with the pizza temporarily forgotten, Sarah gets to work setting up a little geode-cracking station.

"Okay, I want to catch the water and examine it," she

says as she places a rock to crack the geode on in the bucket. "I'm so curious. Does it smell bad? What does it taste like?"

"You're absolutely *not* drinking that water."

She scrunches up her nose at me. "Spoil sport."

"We have to draw the line somewhere. Okay, what do you need me to do?"

She shrugs her gorgeous shoulder and purses her lips. "I honestly don't know. I've never broken one open before."

"Well, we're both beginners, then. That's kind of cool."

"In a really, *really* nerdy sort of way."

I lift her chin so she looks in my eyes, and the excitement there makes me smile.

"You're the sexiest nerd I've ever met, pretty girl."

"Aw. You're sweet. Okay, don't distract me with your sexy ways. I'm discovering treasure here."

"Sorry. You're just irresistible."

"I know." She laughs now and sets the geode on the rock, then braces the chisel on it and takes a whack with the hammer.

It doesn't break.

"I guess it's going to take a few hits," she mutters, and proceeds to hit the hell out of the end of the chisel, until finally, the geode falls into two pieces, and water splashes into the bottom of the bucket.

"Yes!" She flings her hands over her head and dances the cutest little jig I've ever seen in my life. "You know, that's really good exercise. And a way to get out some aggression. I should do it more often."

"Do you ever find these on our beach?"

"No, it's too sandy. Not a lot of rocks. But I think there are places closer to us that we can check out. People pay a lot of money for these. Not that I'll sell *mine*, but I'm just saying."

She picks up one side and examines the crystals that sparkle in the sunlight.

"Looks like quartz. So pretty!"

Then she goes about checking the water. Smelling it, examining it.

"I feel like you need a white coat and a microscope."

"Oh, good idea. I'll buy one of those for the tool kit."

It's LATE when she turns to me in the dark and wraps her sweet body around me like a blanket.

The best blanket that's ever been invented.

We've been sleeping with the back doors of the van open so we can see the view in the moonlight. The cat doesn't seem to mind living in her harness and leash, and is curled up in her little nook by our heads.

"Are you sleeping?" Sarah whispers in my ear as her hand journeys down my naked chest, over my stomach, and cups the family jewels.

"Not anymore," I reply with a grin and kiss her soft lips. She moans, then silently slides on top of me, already wet and inviting me inside her. "Ah, babe."

"I just want you," she says as she braces her hands on my chest and begins to ride me. The night breeze feels amazing against my skin as she moves, her curves lit up by the moonlight. "I don't even care if someone could see."

"No one can see." I sit up and wrap my arms around her, kissing her collarbones and neck. "Jesus Christ, you do things to me."

"Good." Her smile is smug and satisfied as she grinds herself against me. "Because same."

Her mouth drops open when I slide my hand between us and press on her clit with my thumb.

"Come, baby. Don't be quiet."

"The doors are open," she insists, but I shake my head.

"No one's around. No one can hear you." I push just a little harder, and her head falls back on a gasp. She bites that plump lower lip, and when she tightens around me, I take a nipple in my mouth and tug.

"Ah, shit." Her voice is almost guttural, and finally, she comes apart, crying out my name.

To my surprise, she slides off me and turns around, exposing that perfect ass.

"From behind." She pushes her hair out of her face and looks back at me, leaving no room for argument. "Hard."

And hard is what she gets. I slam into her, then slap her ass, sending the sound out into the night. My hand braces over her sacrum, just above her crack, and I ride her hard and fast, our bodies slapping together.

When she cries out once more, and her hands fist in the bedding, I lean over and press my lips to her ear.

"You're *mine*. Do you understand?"

"Yes!" She pushes back on me. "Fuck, yes."

"Mine, and only mine. I'm the only one who gets to touch you like this. To *fuck* you like this."

"Oh, God."

She reaches down and presses her fingers to her clit, and when she tightens even more, I can't hold back.

I jerk and push, gripping her round hips so hard I know I'll leave marks after, and I don't fucking care.

When her breathing slows, she looks back at me, her eyes shining in the moonlight.

"Holy shit, that was fun."

I pull out of her and turn her onto her back, then push inside once more.

"Let's do it again."

"I CAN'T BELIEVE you talked me into a hike."

It's our last morning at the campsite, and I'm milking every damn minute out of it.

"It's a short one," I remind her for the third time. "And it'll be worth it."

"I could be sleeping in the hammock," she mutters, making me smile. I've loved spending all this time with her, just the two of us. Getting to know her again, in every way, is an adventure.

I don't plan to ever stop learning her.

"Trust me, you want to see this."

"I trust you." She reaches back and takes my hand. "I just don't like to hike."

"And yet, you walk the beach pretty much every single day."

"That's not the same," she insists. "That's taking a *walk*."

"What do you think we're doing right now? We're just walking, you know."

"Uphill," she replies. "We're walking *uphill*. Which means it's hiking."

I laugh and urge her on. "It's not much farther. You're doing great."

Ten minutes later, we walk around a bend, and before us is a waterfall. It has to be a hundred feet high, and when the water hits the pool below, it sends up a fine misty spray, making the whole area feel cool and fresh.

"Wow," Sarah breathes and stares with her mouth open, taking it all in. "Okay, this is really cool."

"Told you." I lead her to a log, and we sit next to each other, staring at the water. "Thanks for taking this week with me."

"Are you kidding?" She leans in and kisses my cheek. "Thanks for bringing me. I don't remember the last time I felt this relaxed. I didn't realize I needed it so badly."

"When was the last time you took a vacation?"

She opens her mouth, then closes it again and narrows her eyes, thinking.

"That long, huh?"

"I don't remember," she finally admits. "So, yeah, this

was way overdue. We shouldn't wait a decade between time off."

I shake my head, already mentally planning something for a few months from now. "We shouldn't wait a *year*."

"I don't know how much vacation time you have," she says dryly, "but I don't have a ton."

"You're about to be self-employed," I remind her. "That comes with some liberties."

"Hey, you're right. I'll have to check with the boss, but I hear she's really cool." She laughs and bumps my shoulder with hers. "Yeah, we can travel a little, if you want to."

"I want to." I wrap my arm around her shoulders and pull her against me, kissing her hair and breathing her in.

When she shivers with a chill, I stand and take her hand in mine. "Let's go back to the van and pack up to go home."

"It's time," she agrees, but takes a moment to look back at the waterfall, taking in a deep breath of fresh air. She looks so happy, so calm, and absolutely beautiful. "But first, we have to *hike*."

"You can do it. I have faith."

She grumbles a little, but heading down doesn't take nearly as long as hiking in did, and before I know it, we're back at the van.

"What's that?" Sarah asks, pointing to the side door. "It wasn't there earlier."

"Dirt." I wave it off, but when I approach, I scowl. "Wait, it's a *dent*."

Sure enough, the sliding door of the van has a dent in it the size of my head. No paint is chipped, and it looks like it would be an easy fix, but *how?*

"How in the world did that happen?" she asks, echoing my own thoughts. "We haven't been anywhere in days, and no one has been here."

I prop my hands on my hips and look around the campsite, but nothing has been disturbed. The hammock's floating in the breeze, and our folding chairs sit by the fire pit, all as they were when we left earlier, only an hour ago.

"Weird," I murmur. "I wonder if it could be a bear?"

"A *bear?*" Her voice just raised three octaves. "A freaking *bear?* There aren't bears in Oregon."

I frown over at her. "Of course, there are. Okay, you just lost some science cred with that remark."

"But, there can't be."

"Why not?"

"Because I'm terrified of bears, and I'd know if they were here! Crap. Now I have to be scared of getting eaten by a damn bear. It's good that I didn't know that when we got here, or I would have spent the whole week inside with Petunia. Petunia!"

She races to open the van door, and there's the cat, taking a leisurely bath in the driver's seat.

"She's fine," I assure her. "Come on, let's clean up and gather our stuff, then hit the road."

"There could be a bear lurking behind any of these trees."

"I don't think they lurk." I untie one end of the

hammock. "I'm pretty sure they just go about living their bear life."

"Eating unsuspecting campers," she adds, quickly gathering and folding our chairs. She stows them in the van.

With the fear of becoming a wild bear's lunch, Sarah moves fast, and we get everything packed up and ready to go in less than thirty minutes.

On the way through the campground, Sarah points to the spot, now empty, where the pregnant girl was staying.

"I didn't notice earlier, but she's gone."

"I'm just relieved that neither of us had to deliver a baby this week."

"No kidding. I hope she's okay, though. She was so young and *so* pregnant."

When I stop at the kiosk to check out, I point to the spot on the van that's dented. "Any idea what might have caused that? We found it after we took a little hike this morning."

The man scowls at it, then shakes his head. "I've heard that there's been a black bear hanging around," he says. "Could have been that, trying to get into your food. It also could have been a deer, or anything, really."

"That's what I thought." I nod and sign the checkout paperwork. "Probably wildlife."

"I hope y'all enjoyed your stay."

"We did, thanks."

I nod and drive off, headed toward home.

"Shouldn't they alert people that there's been a bear about?"

"I suspect that they assume anyone who's camping knows that they're taking the chance that there might be any kind of wildlife around."

"I suppose." She bites her lip. "Oh well, we survived the attack. Wait until I tell the others."

I stare over at her and then turn my eyes to the road again, and I laugh my ass off.

"I can't wait to hear how you spin this."

"So, you're telling us that you survived a *bear* attack," June says, narrowing her eyes.

"A bear likely dented the van, yes."

"But you didn't see the bear," Apollo adds.

We're sitting out on my patio, telling camping stories. Not an hour after we arrived home, friends started showing up.

Luna and Wolfe were first, followed closely by June and then Apollo.

I guess they missed us this week.

"We didn't see the bear with our own two eyes," Sarah concedes and reaches for one of the sandwiches that Luna brought with her. "But the ranger said that there had been one about, and what else could have left that dent in the van? It was huge. Poor Petunia was probably scared to death."

"Aside from wild, carnivorous animals," June cuts in. "Did you have fun?"

"So much fun. But enough about us. What's been

going on around here? I didn't hear from anyone, so I figured everything was okay, but my phone has been screwy."

Wolfe frowns at Sarah. "What's wrong with your phone?"

"Who knows?" Sarah shrugs. "I'll probably have to go down to Newport to have it checked out. But I have a shiny new car, so I can go do that whenever I want."

"But not by yourself," June says before I can. "Because if your phone doesn't work and something happens, you need to be able to call for help."

"I'm just destined never to have any alone time again," Sarah mutters. "Anyway, what's been going on?"

"Nothing exciting," Luna replies, earning a scowl from June.

"Are you *kidding* me?" June demands. "We started on the trim inside the inn. The floors are done, at least on the first floor. And the outside is being painted. All of that isn't just exciting, it's"—she waves her hands about, as if she's searching the word—"remarkable."

"Well, yes, there's that," Luna clarifies as I look over to Wolfe. He's just watching her with big ole heart eyes. I wonder if he's told her about the charity race he wants to do yet. "But I meant that there wasn't any *gossip*. That's all. Geez, don't get testy."

"Let's go get some beers," I suggest to the guys, and the three of us leave the girls to chat and go inside. "Any word about who could be trying to get to Sarah?"

"I've been in touch with Cullen since you've been gone," Apollo says. "So far, they don't have much to go on. And there's been no new activity since last week. No one tried to get into the house while you were gone, from what we can tell."

"I tried to do some digging on the ex," Wolfe adds, his face grim. "From everything I can find on him, and there's plenty, he's a ruthless asshole. Didn't do much of anything to actually make his money. He came into it the old-fashioned way. He inherited it."

"Sarah mentioned that he worked really hard."

"At his golf game, maybe," Wolfe says with a shrug. "I don't see where he actually works a job. He doesn't hide the fact that he sleeps around, and about a month after their divorce was final, he remarried. She's ridiculously young."

"He likes them young," I mutter. "Well, thanks for checking."

"From what I can see, he's a prick, but he's not the type to harass her. I don't think he'd know how, and if he's already remarried and focused on that, I doubt he'd come looking for Sarah."

"You're probably right." I nod and open the beer, taking a sip. "Hey, did you ever tell Luna about that race you want to do?"

He opens his mouth to answer, when we hear behind us, "What fucking race?"

Chapter Fifteen

Sarah

"Whoa!" June yelps when the wind takes her hat clean off her head and blows it down the beach. "I guess I didn't need that hat anymore."

"I think it's time to take this party inside." I pick up the plate of sandwiches and my drink. "Looks like we might get a spring storm."

"We could use some rain. It's been *such* a dry spring," Luna adds as we walk inside, just in time to hear Tanner ask Wolfe a question.

"Hey, did you ever tell Luna about that race you want to do?"

June and I look at each other, and Luna erupts with, "What fucking race?"

"I take it that's a no," Apollo says and sips his beer. "Oops."

"What race, Wolfe?"

The man in question rubs the back of his neck and

looks grim as he turns to his fiancée. "It's a *charity* race, Luna."

"Yeah, well, a *charity* race ended your career, so that doesn't make me feel any better."

"Shit," Wolfe mutters and walks to the windows.

"Should we leave for this conversation?" June asks me.

"Hell no," Apollo answers. "I want to watch them fight. We should make popcorn."

"You're such a toddler," June grumbles, but none of us look away from Wolfe and Luna as they square off.

"I haven't agreed to it," Wolfe continues.

"You haven't even breathed a word about it to me," Luna replies. "But apparently, your buddies know. Do the girls know, too? Are they expected to keep it a secret until you can find the right time to break it to me? Probably while we're having sex or something, when you can sneak something by me."

"Jesus." He paces away from her and then back again. "No. Look, it's a race in Miami that sounded like fun. I miss racing, Luna. I've never kept that a secret."

"You *can't* race." She grips his shirt in her fists, and her eyes plead with him as she speaks. It makes my heart hurt for my sweet friend. "You absolutely can*not,* under any circumstances, race a car. It could kill you, and if that happened, I'd be so mad at you, I'd kill you again."

"I didn't tell you because I likely won't get clearance to do it anyway, so there's no reason to upset you. It's a moot point."

"No, it's not, because if a doctor did lose her mind

and say, *Oh, okay, you can race*, you'd actually freaking *do it*. Admit it."

"Oh, yeah, I'd fucking do it in a goddamn heartbeat and wouldn't think twice about it."

Luna shakes her head and releases his shirt, stepping back from him. "After everything you've been through, and everything we're trying to build together, you'd risk your life just to drive a car?"

"*Just* to drive a car?" He crosses his arms over his chest, and I cringe.

That was the wrong thing to say.

"What, exactly, do you think I did for a living, Luna? Drive a fucking taxi? Because trust me, no one's giving taxi drivers three million dollars when they win, or a Ferrari because it's part of their contract."

"*Three million*," I whisper to Tanner, who nods, not taking his eyes off of our friends. "Whoa."

"No, that's not what I meant." Luna's clearly frustrated as she pushes her hands through her dark hair. "I meant that you're willing to throw away so much for the sake of driving a car."

"Is that an ultimatum?" he asks, his voice suddenly very cold.

I sidle over and slip my hand into Tanner's, and he gives it a squeeze.

"Not only can I not watch you race ever again, but I *won't*, Wolfe. The thought of losing you that way keeps me up at night and fuels my nightmares, so if you think that I'd willingly live through it with you, you're crazy."

"So, if I say yes, we're through? You'll walk out on me, and that's it for us?"

"The fact that you'd even consider saying yes, and that you kept this from me, has me questioning some things right now, if I'm being honest."

"Fuck that, Luna."

"No," she says, shaking her head emphatically. "I practically *carried* you up the cliffs by my house, more than once, because you couldn't manage it on your own. You black out for hours. You're in so much pain it takes my own breath away, and you're telling me that you'd consider doing the one thing that could fucking *kill* you?"

"It's like breathing," he hisses, and takes her shoulders in his hands. "Don't you get it? It's my goddamn lifeblood, and it was torn away from me. I didn't get to choose that."

"You can choose it now," she says, her face suddenly ashen. "You're in control now. Wolfe, you *know* you can't do this."

He blows out a shaky breath and then yanks Luna into his arms and hugs her close.

"I just wish I could have it back, just for a little while, so I could say goodbye to it in my own way."

"I know." She rubs soothing circles over his back. "I know, and I'm so damn sorry. I really am."

June sniffles and wipes away a tear, and I realize I have tears of my own on my cheeks that I swipe away.

It must be torture to lose something that you love so much like that.

"I never planned to accept the invitation," Wolfe

admits as he kisses Luna's head. "I know that I can't. But it felt damn good to be asked."

"Of course, it did." She pats his cheek and then twists his ear.

"Hey!"

"That's for not telling me." Now she pats his cheek again and smiles softly. "I wouldn't really leave you. Probably."

"Good to know."

"I feel like I should pay admission to this show," Apollo says, and Tanner nods.

"At least twenty bucks a person," Tanner agrees.

"Smartasses," Wolfe mutters, but gives us all a smile. "Sorry."

"For what?" June asks. "It was a damn good show. I give it a seven out of ten. By the way, when do I get to drive the Ferrari?"

"Never." Wolfe smirks and reaches for his beer. "You may ride in it. But you'll never drive it. You couldn't handle that car."

"Uh-oh," I mutter as June's eyebrows climb into her hairline, and she blinks at Wolfe for ten full seconds before flipping him the bird.

"I can drive *anything*," she replies and bares her teeth. "Even your fancy car. But that's fine. I don't want to, anyway."

I hide my laugh behind my own glass of water.

"You can't even drive a backhoe," Apollo adds with a smirk. "You'd kill yourself in a muscle car."

June whips around and glares at Apollo.

"If looks could kill," Tanner whispers, and I press my lips together so I don't laugh.

"I missed them," I say, not bothering to whisper now. "All of their drama and quirks keep us on our toes."

"You have plenty of your own drama," Luna reminds me. "And speaking of, have you heard anything about Angela?"

"No." I shake my head. "And I probably won't."

"Right." June nods and then rolls her eyes. "That girl is vindictive. You watch your back."

"If I watch my back any more than I already am, I'll have a permanent kink in my neck."

"For such a nice girl," Apollo says thoughtfully, "you sure have a lot of people who don't like you."

"It's a gift."

"So, I'm hoping that I can cut my hours back to part time. I don't want to quit altogether right now, but I really would like the chance to focus more on my art and explore the possibility of making a living from it."

Gordy's eyes narrow. He always looks so grouchy, but I know that he's just a big teddy bear.

He is with me, anyway.

"You listen to me," he says, shaking his finger at me. "You only get this one life to live, and you have to do whatever it is that makes you feel good. Makes you feel proud. I knew that working for me was just a stopover until you found what that was."

My jaw drops. "You did?"

"Sure. You came home sad, and a little broken, but the important thing is that you came home. You're figuring yourself out, and I'm damn proud of you for that, kid."

He's always called me kid.

"I'm over thirty and just starting to figure myself out."

"Many folks never do, no matter their age, so don't be hard on yourself. You can talk with Sunny and work out a schedule with her. I'll give her a heads-up. Do what makes you happy."

"Thank you." I know it's not terribly professional of me, but I love Gordy, so I cross the space between us and hug him. "You've always been here for me, no matter what, and I can't tell you how much I love and appreciate you, Gordy."

"Don't get too mushy now." He may sound gruff, but his face is soft as he smiles down at me. "Same goes, kid. Now, I have to get back into the kitchen."

The rest of my shift runs smoothly. Sunny and I are able to work out a schedule that works for both of us, and when I bounce out to my car at seven in the evening, I feel excited about the possibility of selling my art.

The sun is just setting when I turn my car toward Tanner's house, but suddenly, the front, left side sags, and I hear an awful flapping sound.

I ease the car to the side of the road, and when I climb out, I scowl at the flat tire.

"Damn it." I kick it, then reach for my phone, but I don't have any service, and I'm definitely not currently on

Wi-Fi. I *really* need to get my phone figured out. "At least I'm not far from home."

I've already been on my feet most of the day, and they're not happy with me, but the walk doesn't take long, and when I'm safely in Tanner's house, he turns to look at me and frowns.

"I didn't hear your car."

"That's because I had a flat tire, and I had to abandon it." I blow out a breath. "Can I please borrow your phone so I can call Wolfe and ask him to tow it?"

"How did you get home?"

"I walked."

His eyes narrow now, and he leans closer, as if he didn't hear me. "I'm sorry, what?"

"I walked, Tanner. It's fine. *I'm* fine. I just need to have my car towed."

"No, it's not fine, Sarah. We agreed that you wouldn't be alone until we figure out who's been breaking into your place."

"What was I supposed to do, wait in my car until someone came to find me? It was less than a mile, and it's not dark yet. I'm fine."

"We're fixing your phone situation first thing tomorrow morning."

"I have to work."

"You need a phone," he counters. His voice is calm, but his eyes are *not*. "This is a safety issue now. So, we'll go to Newport and figure it out tomorrow."

"I don't remember you being this bossy and controlling when I was in high school."

He doesn't answer me. With his eyes pinned to mine, he taps his phone and presses it to his ear. "Hey, Wolfe. Sarah had a flat tire and needs a tow. Do you have a company you use for that? Great. Yeah, she's home now, but the car is parked on the side of the road. Where is it?" he asks me.

"On the corner of Seaside Lane, not too far from Huckleberry Delight."

Tanner relays the information. "Great. Thank you. Just let me know how much it is. Talk to you later."

He ends the call, and I just stand here and stare at him.

"I should have been the one to do that. It's *my* car."

Tanner sits on the couch and leans forward, his elbows braced on his knees.

"I'm so angry right now," he begins, his voice a study in controlled fury, "you might want to watch yourself."

"What, exactly, are you angry about, Tanner? I couldn't just sit in my car. I'd rather walk home than back to Gordy's."

"Something could happen to you." He swallows hard, and his jaw tightens. "And that's not acceptable."

I straddle his lap and frame his face in my hands. "I'm *fine*. I'm not hurt. Flat tires just happen, you know? Maybe I drove over a nail, or maybe the tire just needs to be replaced. It doesn't mean that someone booby-trapped it."

"You don't know that."

"You're becoming paranoid," I inform him as I lean in

to brush his lips softly with my own. "I'm okay. I promise."

His arms loop around me now, almost desperately, and he hugs me close, burying his face in my breasts and holding on tightly.

"There have been too many shitty things happening lately," he says at last. "Just humor me and take the morning off so we can handle your phone."

"Done."

His head comes up in surprise. "That was too easy."

"No, I get it. If the roles were reversed, I'd be freaking out, too. We'll get it fixed, and if something happens to my car again, I'll wait there, with the doors locked, while I call for help."

"Thank you." Some of the tension melts away as he hugs me again. "Now, let's get you naked."

"Naked?" I giggle when he reaches under my shirt and tugs it up and over my head.

"I have some adrenaline to work off."

His hands turn me into goo as he works me over, undressing and exposing me, kissing and teasing me, and when he finally lays me down on the couch and covers me, pressing inside, I think I might go blind from the pleasure of it.

"Holy shit," I mutter when we're a pile of sweaty, panting flesh. "I should get a flat tire more often."

"Absolutely not."

"You KNOW, one of the most annoying things about living in Huckleberry Bay is that it's so far from everything," I say the next morning as we drive through Newport to go to the cell phone store. "There aren't many *easy* errands we can run."

"It's a trade-off, that's for sure." He finds the store and pulls into the parking lot, cutting the engine.

"Let's get this handled," I say and walk in ahead of him. It's early enough in the day that there's no one waiting ahead of us.

"How can I help you?" A man with the name *Justin* on his lapel greets us.

"I'm having phone issues." I explain about not having service, and Justin heads straight for the computer to bring up my account. "Do I just need to replace the phone?"

"You canceled your service with us last week," he says with a scowl.

"I absolutely did *not* cancel my service."

His face is lined with confusion as he taps some keys. "It says here that you came into this store on Wednesday afternoon and canceled your service."

"I was in the woods on Wednesday afternoon," I inform him. "But either way, let's just get it set back up."

"Sure, that should be easy enough." But when he taps some more keys, he loses the smile on his face. "Actually, it says here that you owe about six hundred dollars in fees, and I can't reinstate your plan without you paying that first."

I stare at him, certain I just heard him wrong.

"That's impossible."

"No, there are fees for canceling before your contract is up, and given that you've had this plan for less than a year, the fees are high."

"You've got to be kidding me. I didn't cancel." My heartbeat picks up at the thought of spending that much money on something I didn't do.

"The computer says you did."

"Okay," Tanner says, cutting in. "We won't be paying that today, and we will contest it. In the meantime, add her to my plan."

Justin looks like he wants to argue with that, but then he just shrugs.

"Yeah, okay. I'm probably not supposed to, but I don't care."

"Can I have my old number back, please?"

"I'll see what I can do."

As Justin taps away at the computer, I'm reminded how freaking long it always takes at the cell phone store, and how much I hate it.

Suddenly, Justin sighs. "I'm sorry, I can't give you the number back because it's been assigned to someone else."

"You have *got* to be kidding me," I protest. "Justin, it's been turned off for a couple of days, not weeks or years. They must hold those numbers aside for a little while before reassigning them."

"Usually they do, but if someone requests it, they'll release it."

Tanner's hand on my shoulder tightens.

"Are you telling me that someone requested my number?"

Justin's face pokers up. "I can't give you that information. All I can say is that the number isn't available."

"Fine. Just give me a number, and I'll figure it out."

"Why would someone request my number?" I demand once Tanner and I are back in his vehicle. "It's not special."

"Someone is *really* dicking with you," Tanner replies as he pulls out of the parking lot, his face set in grim lines.

"It's a coincidence," I begin, but when he shoots me a warning look, the one that says he's pissed, I just shrug. "Okay, maybe it is, and maybe it isn't. It's mostly just a pain in the ass."

"It's harassment," he mutters. "I think it's time you got an attorney, Sarah."

"For what? I don't have proof of literally *anything*."

"Then we'll hire a fucking private investigator. We have to do something because I can't just sit back and watch all of this shit happen to you, over and over again. It's not okay, and it has to stop."

"The private investigator isn't a bad idea." I tap my lips with the pad of my finger, thinking it over. "They might be able to dig something up that we haven't."

"I'm glad we see eye to eye on that one."

"Do you *know* any PIs?"

Tanner nods. "As a matter of fact, I do."

July 30, 2018

Dear Diary,

I found out about another affair. This makes six in the past ten years that I know about. Honestly, I just feel dead inside at this point. He doesn't love me. I don't think he ever did. I simply serve a purpose for him.

Obviously not well because he hasn't had sex with me in more than five years and gets it elsewhere.

That doesn't bother me. I have no interest in him physically.

I have no interest in him at all.

But I don't have anywhere else to go. I'm stuck here.

I miss my friends and my brother. And I have so many regrets.

-Sarah

Chapter Sixteen

Tanner

"So, what now?"

The question comes from Scott. I'm having lunch with him at Three Sisters, filling him in on everything that's been happening with his sister.

I have another motive for asking him here, but that'll come later.

"I called Belle Lovejoy," I reply with a shrug and eat my burger. "We're meeting with her at the end of the week."

"A private investigator," Scott says in surprise. "I suppose that makes sense. Maybe Belle can find some answers for us. You know, some of this could just be coincidence. The tire, the phone, things like that. They may not be connected to the break-in at the house at all."

"I know. I thought of that." I set my water glass down and frown at the other man. "But what if they *aren't*? Something just feels so off lately, and I can't explain it. Sure, some of it could just be life kicking her in the balls, but something in my gut doesn't think so. I'd rather be safe than sorry."

"Agreed." He wads up his napkin and tosses it on his empty plate. "How is she? Aside from all the shit that's been going on, I mean, how is she?"

"She's doing better," I reply, knowing exactly what Scott's asking. "She's not so timid and doesn't seem so sad anymore."

"I was kind of surprised when you two started seeing each other," he admits. "Not because it's *you*, but because it seemed so soon after everything that went down last year. But, she has to move on. That's the healthiest thing for her, to move on with her life. To *enjoy* her life, so thanks for being part of that for her, man."

"I waited longer than I wanted to," I admit with a laugh. "You thought it felt fast, but it was the longest few months of my life. I would still be waiting, even with her renting out my guesthouse, if she wasn't ready. She finally approached *me* because she was sick of me twiddling my thumbs."

Scott laughs, nodding. "Good. Good for both of you."

"And that leads me to this." I shift in my seat, suddenly nervous. "I'm going to ask her to marry me."

He doesn't blink. He also doesn't look surprised.

"Are you asking for my blessing?"

"Yeah, I am. You're the only family that she gives a shit about. You may still be trying to figure out your relationship, but she loves you, and you're her brother, so I'm telling you and asking at the same time."

"Look, I know that you love her. You've loved her

since you were a kid. Fucked up a little, but hopefully that's out of your system."

"I fucked up a lot." I blow out a breath. "So it's a wonder to me that she wants anything at all to do with me. I can tell you that I'll always do my best to protect her, to treat her the way she should be treated, and to be a man that she's proud of."

"Good. Because if she ever comes to me and says that you've hurt her in *any* way, I'll light your house on fire and watch it burn to the goddamn ground."

"We understand each other, then."

His lips twitch with humor as I offer him my hand to shake.

"Circling back to what we were talking about earlier, her phone being out of commission explains why I couldn't reach her last week. Mom's ashes arrived, and I spoke with June about burying her. If Sarah's schedule is clear, we might go ahead and do that later today."

"I'll text you her new number." I pick up my phone and send Scott the contact. "I think she's free later, but you should check with her."

"I'm gonna shoot her a text now," his words are slow as he taps on his phone. "I just want to bury that woman and move on."

"What happens when your dad dies?" I wince and then sigh. "I know that sounds bad. I guess I'm curious if you'll bury him with your mom, or—"

"I don't give two shits about what happens to my father, before *or* after he dies," Scott replies shortly. "He can rot in hell as far as I'm concerned."

"Point taken."

His phone dings with a text. "She's free this evening. Good. She also says to tell you that she's running to the grocery store. How...*domestic*."

"It'll happen to you one day. You'll meet a woman and fall flat on your face in love, and then you'll be talking about grocery lists and work schedules and thinking about fucking her all the damn time."

"Hey." He looks pained as he sits back in his seat. "She's my *sister*. I don't want to know about the perverted things you think about."

"She's not complaining, trust me. But it's more than that. It's having the person you like the best there to just be with you. Hang out. Walk the beach, or watch TV. Unload about your day. My point is, it'll happen to you, and then I'll razz you about domestic conversations about the grocery store."

"No, it's not going to happen." He rubs his hand over his hair. "Relationships are too complicated, and I'm pretty much married to the job, so you enjoy your bliss with my sister, and I'll cheer you on."

I want to argue, but my phone rings, and I see that it's Sarah.

"Hey, babe."

"Hey." Just with that one word, I can hear the frustration in her voice.

"What's wrong?"

"Well, I just came out to start my car to go to the grocery store, and it's out of gas. Like, *completely* out. There aren't even enough fumes to get me to the gas station. Tanner, am I going crazy? Because I could have sworn that I just fueled up the other day."

"You did." I meet Scott's eyes with my own. "You put gas in after Wolfe took care of the tire. I'll deal with it."

"I'm so annoyed," she mutters. "I couldn't have used a full tank in less than a week."

"We'll figure it out. I'm on my way."

"Thanks. Sorry to interrupt your guy lunch."

"We were just wrapping it up. No worries. I'll see you in a few."

I hang up and scowl.

"What happened?" Scott asks.

"She's out of gas. She had at least half a tank in that car. What the hell is going on?"

Scott blows out a breath. "I'm coming with you. We'll see if there's any damage to the car."

"Let's go."

Scott follows me to my place and parks behind me in the driveway. Sarah's standing by her car, her face filled with frustration and confusion.

"All I want to do is go buy some bananas," she says when I get out of the car. "So they can get overly ripe, and I can try my hand at making banana bread. That's all. Why is that so much to ask?"

"She's getting a little crazy," Scott murmurs.

"I'm *not* crazy, except I feel that way all the time now. Anyway, the stupid car is out of gas. I've barely been able to drive it since I got it."

Scott squats by the gas tank as I pull Sarah into my arms for a long, firm hug. "It's okay. Maybe you didn't fill it up all the way the other day. Sometimes the pump kicks off before the tank is full, and I just stop filling it, thinking that it's done."

"Maybe," she says with a sigh. "It's entirely possible that happened because I've had a lot on my mind lately."

"I don't see where anything has been tampered with," Scott adds as he stands. "Doesn't look like anyone pried the tank open or anything like that. You probably just didn't fill it up all the way, like Tanner said."

"So annoying." Sarah props her hands on her hips. "Now I need a ride to the grocery store because I'm going to want that banana bread in a few days."

"You know, you can make the bread without waiting for them to go black," Scott says.

"But the bread is better when they *are* overripe."

"Says the woman who doesn't like to cook." I laugh when she scowls at me. "I'm sure it'll be delicious, pretty girl."

"Just like the mac 'n' cheese and hotdogs," Scott adds.

"You guys can make fun of me all you want." She lifts her little nose into the air and sniffs. "I don't care. I won't share my freshly baked banana bread with you."

"Now you're just being mean," Scott says and reaches out to tug on her blonde hair. "You'll share with me. I'm your favorite."

"*Least* favorite brother today." She grins at him, though. "Okay, you're my favorite again."

"*Yes.*" He pumps his hand in the air triumphantly. "Okay, I'm gonna head out. I'll see you later at June's."

"Bye," Sarah says with a wave. "How about it? Shall we go to the store?"

"Yes. We have that meeting with the art customer in an hour, as well."

"I didn't forget." She chews her lip. "You know what, on second thought, let me go in and change really quick so we can go to the store and then straight to the gallery."

"I'm fine with that."

***

"I'M SO DAMN NERVOUS." Sarah adjusts the collar of her red blouse for the fourth time since we arrived at the gallery.

"Don't be." I kiss her forehead and then adjust one of the canvases so the lighting hits the center of the piece just right. "All of these are incredible."

"He's right," Wayne says from behind us, admiring Sarah's art. "These are really beautiful, and so unlike anything else we have in the gallery. They're an excellent addition to our exhibit."

"Now you guys are just flattering me."

"I don't flatter unless it's earned." I kiss her forehead once more. "And it is. She should be here any minute."

And I'm not wrong.

A few moments later, Clementine Bodine walks through my door, a bright smile on her beautiful face, and she hurries over to me and plants a kiss right on my lips.

"Tanner, *darling*," she says with excitement. "It's always just an absolute joy to see you. God, you're gorgeous. Let's have a replay of that weekend in Hawaii sometime soon, shall we?"

"Uh, Clem, this is Sarah Pedersen." I step out of Clem's reach and turn to find fire sparking in Sarah's eyes. "She's the artist I was telling you about and the reason I called you in today."

"Damn," Clem says and looks me up and down. "A girl can try, I suppose. Hello, Sarah, it's a pleasure to finally meet you. Tanner has told me about your work, and I'm excited to see it today."

"Thank you," Sarah says with a smile that doesn't reach her eyes. "We have some pieces on display for your perusal."

"Oh, Tanner," Clem exclaims as she approaches the canvases. "You weren't kidding. These are amazing, and I can already picture them in several rooms in my house. Oh, and this one of the sailboat would be divine for my brother's new place. He's building a house on the hills, overlooking the ocean. Did you hear?"

"I think I did hear that," I reply with a nod. "I'm sure that would make a great housewarming gift."

"I'll take them all," Clem says, and Sarah's head snaps back as if she's been slapped.

"I'm sorry, what?"

"I want all six of them. Can I take them today?" She turns to me. "I'd also like to have them hung in the house, as we've done in the past."

"Wayne can handle that," I reply with a nod, and Clem's eyes go to ice.

"I see." Her gaze shifts between me and Sarah, and I reach for Sarah's hand. "So, that's how it is."

"Yes, Clem. That's how it is. But you're a loyal and dear customer, and I wanted to give you the first opportunity to buy these pieces before they go on display or are offered to anyone else."

Clem turns back to the paintings and nods slowly. "I do love them, and I'm still taking them all, even if I don't get to have sex with you ever again."

I feel my face wanting to flush, so I swallow, willing the flush away.

I fucked up. I should have told Sarah more about this customer, but it didn't occur to me at the time. Clem is in the past, and Sarah's all I think about now.

"I'm pleased that you like my work," Sarah says, her voice all cool professionalism. "And I appreciate your business."

"But you don't appreciate my interest in Tanner."

"I've been in love with Tanner since I was fourteen," Sarah responds. "So, no. I don't appreciate it. But, I can respect it, because he's handsome and just generally wonderful. The only way you and I will have an issue, Ms. Bodine, is if you think you're going to try to poach him from me."

"Oh, honey, I don't poach." Clem's smile is genuine as she turns to me. "Now that I know that you're off the market, I can stop spending so much fucking money on art."

My jaw drops, and both women laugh.

"Do you think I need to change out all of the art in

my house twice a year?" she continues. "I may be rich, but I'm not foolish. There's a race car driver in town that I've heard is delicious."

"He's taken, too," Sarah says helpfully. "By my best friend."

"Well, shit. If you hear of anyone *on* the market, be sure to let me know." She winks at Sarah and then turns to me. "Bill me for the art and for the install."

"I will," I assure her, and slide my hands in my pockets as she walks out of the gallery. "I'm in big trouble, aren't I?"

"When was Hawaii?" Sarah asks.

"Two years ago."

"When was the last time you fucked her?"

I hear Wayne choke on a laugh, but I ignore him.

"Two years ago."

"Why didn't you tell me that she would practically make out with you when she walked through the door so I was prepared and didn't have to physically restrain myself from knocking her ass through a wall?"

I swallow my own laugh now.

"Well, she doesn't always do that."

"Right," Wayne says. "She flirts mercilessly. But since you came back to town, Sarah, Tanner doesn't pay her any attention. Hell, he hasn't encouraged her in a long ass time."

"She was a distraction for a little while." My voice is low so only Sarah can hear. "And who knew that she didn't really want to buy all new artwork every few months?"

"Uh, a blind man could have seen that," Sarah replies and pats my cheek. "You're oblivious. And that's the reason why you're not in deep trouble. So, how much are we charging her for all of this?"

"No less than three thousand each."

Sarah goggles at me. "What? Three thousand *each*?"

"Should be more," Wayne calls out.

"You're a new artist, still unknown. We'll start there and increase as word gets out. Clem is getting a hell of a bargain."

"Holy shit," Sarah whispers. "That's a lot of money."

"Congratulations," Wayne says as he approaches us with champagne and flutes. "You need to celebrate your first ever sale."

"I'm proud of you," I tell her and take a sip of the bubbly.

"I'm kind of proud of me, too," she says and sips her own glass. "I have so much work to do."

"It's a drug, isn't it?" Wayne asks. "There can't be anything else like it."

"I think I'll be painting full time by the end of the year," Sarah replies. "As long as they keep selling, that is."

A customer walks through the door and makes a slow circle through the gallery. When he sees the collection of easels set up behind us, and the artwork on them, his eyebrows pinch together.

"Are these available?"

I grin down at Sarah, whose mouth just dropped wide open, and turn to the man.

"These have been purchased, but this is the artist, and I believe she has more work to come."

He turns to Sarah and offers to shake her hand. "Do you take on commissions? If I wanted a particular view painted or some such thing? I understand that would cost more, of course."

"Sure, I could probably do that from a photo."

"Would you be willing to visit the place so you can see it firsthand?"

"Depending on how far away it is, I don't see why not."

He looks back at the other work and then smiles at Sarah. "My wife's birthday is coming up, and I do believe I just found the perfect gift for her."

"How exciting," Sarah replies. "I'll give you my email address, and we will work out the details."

"Wonderful. Oh, she's just going to love this."

The two exchange information, and when he's gone, Sarah just stares at me, as if she can't believe it.

"I think you'd better have business cards made," I inform her.

"We also need to do a show," Wayne says from the counter. "Perhaps for the holidays?"

"I don't even know what that means," Sarah says, but then launches herself into my arms and hugs me close. "Who knew that I could do this?"

"I did." I kiss her softly. "I knew, pretty girl. I'm proud of you. And this is only the beginning."

"I need supplies," she says. "And I'd like to start

painting out in the guesthouse again. I *like* painting out there."

"We'll figure it out," I assure her, thrilled to see her so full of passion for her art. "You have to work where it feels right."

"With you." She says it with a whisper and tips her forehead against my own. "It feels right with you."

I couldn't agree more.

Chapter Seventeen

Sarah

"I don't know what to say." I'm standing next to Scott, who's holding my hand, as we stare down at the hole in the ground. Scott called the city and got the information for the correct way to do this, so he dug the hole before I got here.

Thank God, there wasn't someone else buried in this exact location. Grandma must be a little to the left.

Or the right.

How should I know?

"We don't have to say anything," is his reply. "We can just drop her down there and cover her up."

"That seems cold, even for her." I breathe in deeply and look around the small graveyard. "You know, it's never scared me to be out here. It's not creepy at all."

I look down at the simple, plastic box that Mom's remains came in. It fits her. She was always simple and didn't have nice things.

If she did, she sold them for drugs.

"You were a shitty mother," I say at last. "Probably the worst one I know of. Maybe not the worst in history, but pretty fucking horrible. You let your babies suffer and watched them be hungry. Hurt. Beaten by their own father. You were selfish, mean, and an all-around bitch."

"Don't hold back," Scott mutters, but he chuckles.

"Oh, there's no need to hold back." I sigh and lean my head on my brother's shoulder. "All we ever wanted was for them to love us."

"Yeah, well, that didn't happen. And there's no need to stand here and be sad about it. To be sad about her dying."

"I'm not sad." I look at the other headstones around us again. "I bet that most of these people had loved ones who cried over their graves when they died. They had flowers and people who grieved for them."

"Probably," he agrees.

"I think the saddest part of this is that literally no one in the world gives a shit that Melissa Pedersen is dead. No one grieves for her. She'll be buried here, without a stone, and when you and I are gone, no one will even remember that she lived."

"A waste." His voice is hard. "She was a waste of human flesh."

"I'm so glad that it's not me." Tears come now, and they run unchecked down my cheeks. "If I'd stayed with Anthony, when my time came, no one would care. He made sure of that. Yes, Mom's situation is different because it's her own doing, but Christ, Scott, I'm glad it's not me."

"No one wants to imagine this." He shakes his head slowly. "That when they're gone, no one will care. It's pathetic. And like you said, it's her own doing. Had she been a decent fucking human, she'd have all of Huckleberry Bay here to say their goodbyes. She didn't give a shit about anyone here, including us."

"No. She didn't. So, I hope you finally rest easy, Mom, because God knows that you weren't restful when you were here."

I squat and place her box in the ground, and then Scott covers her up. I place a single red rose over the grave, and then we step away and walk toward our cars.

"We won't do this for Dad," Scott says, his voice firm. "Tanner asked me about it earlier, and I want to make it clear to you that if and when we ever get the call that he's finally dead, they can keep his damn remains. I don't care what they do with him, but he's not coming here, and we aren't doing this for him."

"No." I shake my head and then turn to my brother and give him a kiss on the cheek. "We won't do this for him. I'm sorry they hurt you, Scott."

"Hurt both of us." He jerks his shoulder. "And we lived through it. Maybe we're better because of them. Despite them."

"Maybe." I lean on the car and look up at the chapel. "Took me a long time to come to terms with the fact that I deserve to be loved, though. A really long damn time. And I'm not convinced that you're there yet."

"Let's not psychoanalyze ourselves today." He

reaches up and ruffles my hair. "What are your plans this weekend?"

"I have a girls' night thing tonight at Luna's. Gonna eat a bunch of food and drink some drinks."

"Call me if you need a ride. I'm gonna go to Lighthouse Pizza with the guys and collect their money at pool."

"Looks like we're both going to blow off some steam tonight. I think that's good. Have fun, and let me know if *you* need a ride."

He grins and reaches for his door handle. "I don't plan to go home alone tonight."

"I don't need to know that."

He laughs and waits for me to get in my car to drive away. Before I pull away from the curb, I take one last look toward the small grave.

"Goodbye, Mom."

I'm the last to arrive at Luna's. It took me a while to decide what to wear, and then Tanner wanted to make out in the closet, and really, who can resist that?

Not me.

So, when I pull up to the lighthouse, I'm not surprised to find several cars already parked by the main house.

I let myself in and find Luna and June, along with Cordelia, Mira, and Darla from Three Sisters Kitchen, all in Luna's kitchen, just setting out a spread of food.

"I'm so glad I'm not too late for all of this deliciousness."

Their heads all turn to me, and then they welcome me in a way that is so special, and it is something I hadn't felt in more than a decade before I moved back home last year.

I belong here. This is my home, with this community of people, and I love it *so much*.

"What's on the menu?" I ask.

"We're trying out even *more* things for the inn's menu," Mira informs me with a smile that lights up all of Oregon. "I keep finding new things, thinking up new recipes, and I want to use them all, so we've decided to offer a rotating menu, with a few staples that will be available all the time. Tonight, we're starting with the staples."

"I love staples," I say and dance a little jig. "And I love your cooking, so I can't wait for this. Did you give them a tour of the inn, Luna?"

"Not yet," she says. "We were waiting for you."

"Oh, you didn't have to. I've seen it."

"You're going to want to see this," June says with a wink. "But first, food."

I go to grab some ChapStick out of my purse, but when I pull it out, it's completely empty.

Like it's been broken off.

"Okay, you guys. Little things have been happening lately that totally irritate me. Like, I forget that I was out of something and don't replace it. Or things are in different places than I remember putting them. Is this memory loss menopause? I'm in the middle of menopause, aren't I?"

"I don't think menopause happens in your early thirties," Darla says. "So I don't think it's that."

"Ugh, I'm so sick of this. This morning, I went to finish the painting I did for Tanner, and my brushes were moved. Then, I went to start my car, and all of my gas was gone, and I'm sure it wasn't on empty. Just now, this ChapStick is gone. Like, I broke it off at some point, but I have absolutely no recollection of doing that."

"Maybe you should see a doctor," Mira suggests.

"It could just be stress," June points out. "You've had a lot going on, Sarah."

"That's true." I sigh, but then grin when Mira slides a plate loaded with apple turnovers. "We're starting with dessert?"

"We're starting with *breakfast*," she says and passes plates to the others. "This will be a breakfast option every day. It's easy for guests to take on the go or to grab as a morning snack."

"Holy shit, I just had an orgasm," June moans, and I laugh but totally agree with her.

"These are *divine*." I wipe my mouth with my napkin and take another bite. "So buttery and light. And the apple filling is just the right amount."

"Does it need more brown sugar?"

"No!" we all exclaim in unison.

For the next hour, we devour everything from the turnovers to turkey sandwiches and so many other delicious things that my stomach doesn't know what to do with itself when we're finally finished.

"I may never walk again," Luna says, patting her stomach. "That was delicious."

"Wait until next time, when I show off the seasonal and rotation recipes," Mira promises with a satisfied smile. "Now, let's go see the inn and daydream, shall we?"

"Yes, let's walk off all of those calories," I agree.

The walk from Luna's house to the inn only takes a few minutes, and once inside, June flips on the lights.

"There's paint," I say in surprise when I see the pretty light blues on the walls that accent the white.

"There's still a *lot* of work to do," June says, then looks around, taking it all in. "But we're coming along, and it'll be done by this fall, like Luna wants."

"What's that rag on the wall?" I ask, pointing just left of the main entrance.

June and Luna share a smile.

"Why don't you take the rag down?" Luna suggests.

"Uh, okay." I eye my friends as they all share a look, and then I pull on the rag, uncovering a plaque.

Three young girls played and dreamed here.
Luna, who is the lighthouse and inn keeper.
June, who built the inn with her own two hands.
And Sarah, who created all of the paintings in the guest rooms.
Three best friends, whose love will always be a piece of Luna's Light.

I READ it twice and then feel two sets of arms wrap around me from behind in a tight hug.

"I'm so grateful," I whisper through the tears. "So grateful that I'm home and that I have the two of you in my life. You're my family."

"Same goes," June says and kisses my cheek.

I smell roses fill the room and glance over at Luna. "Do you smell her?"

"Hell, we can all smell her," Cordelia says from behind us.

"She's happy," Luna says. "I think she loves having so many of us here, and that we're making this place something special."

A door gently closes upstairs.

"Looks like you're right," I reply. "She talks to me a lot when I'm in here alone, painting. She doesn't say *words,* but I smell and hear her. I know what she's trying to say."

"Me, too," June says. "She's here often when we're working."

"Us, as well," Mira adds. "But she never tries to scare us. I think she's just here to see what we're doing and to be a small part of it. This was her home, and I hope she thinks that we're respectful and doing something she would be proud of."

The door closes again, harder this time.

"See? She talks." I laugh and wipe away the last of

the tears. "That's the sweetest thing I've ever seen, you guys. Thank you for including me."

"Your heart is in here as much as ours is," June says. "You should be included. And I think guests will find it to be a sweet anecdote to read when they check in."

"You're right." I turn to the three sisters. "Now, let's check out the kitchen."

"We thought you'd never ask," Darla says and leads the way down the hall, toward the back of the inn, where the kitchen sits.

There will be double doors that lead out to an amazing patio where guests can sit outside and enjoy the view of the water.

And the kitchen...Mira's kitchen is just *gorgeous*.

"Countertops will be installed in two weeks," June informs us as I walk around the giant island in the middle of the room.

"There's so much countertop space here for you, Mira," Luna says. "Once it's installed, that is."

"I can bake and chop and do all the things without worrying about space," Mira agrees. "Oh, and my stand mixer will be hidden in a cabinet that will pop up when I need it. It's *so* cool."

"Oh, speaking of hidden things," June says, snapping her fingers. "I have to show Luna and Sarah something in the next few days at the chapel. No rush, I just found some cool stuff."

"Love that," I reply on my way to the double doors. I open them and step outside, breathing in the salty ocean air. Water hits the cliffs with high tide and sends sprays up into the air.

It's always dramatic. Always gorgeous.

"It's such a special place, Luna." She takes my hand as she joins me out here. "You're going to be full all the time. People will flock here. I think it's wonderful, and Huckleberry Bay will only be better for it."

"I hope so," she says with a long, deep breath. "Because if the community hates it, I'm screwed."

"No one will hate it." I lean my head on her shoulder. "It's way too cool to hate it."

"Hey, you guys," June says from the doorway. "Let's go drink some martinis. Darla brought all the fixin's for them."

"Oh, that sounds lovely." Hand in hand, Luna and I turn for the door. "I need a drink."

"Why aren't you ladies dating?" I ask once we all have a concoction in our hands, and we're sitting in Luna's living room. "All three of you are gorgeous, smart, and wonderful."

"We're also incredibly busy," Cordelia says.

"Not to mention, no one has really asked us out on a date. At least, they haven't asked *me*," Mira adds with a shrug. "Besides, I've got my head in the kitchen too much to go out and chase down a man."

"Well, if none of you are snatched up, the men in this town are blind," June adds.

"What about *you*?" Darla asks, looking right at June. "You're single."

"And happy to stay that way," June insists.

"But, what about orgasms?" This comes from Luna, who's clearly been enjoying the martinis. Her eyes are a little glassy, and her mouth is soft as she grins. "A girl needs regular orgasms."

"Who says she needs a man for that?" June demands. "There are plenty of other ways to get to that goal."

We all blink at June for a moment and then erupt in laughter.

"I suppose that's true," I reply. "Hell, I went more than eight years without sex."

"What?" Cordelia frowns. "But, weren't you married?"

"Marriage has absolutely *nothing* to do with sex," I assure her. "He got tired of me after a while, and when I found out that he was screwing everything with a set of lungs and a heartbeat, I knew that I'd never let him touch me again. Who knows what he was exposed to?"

"Ew," Mira says, wrinkling her nose. "That sucks big time."

"Not really." I shrug and take a sip of this excellent beverage. "He was really, *really* bad at it, anyway. I don't think he ever made me come. So, I wasn't missing out on much. Now, Tanner, on the other hand, never has an issue getting me to come."

"Here's the good stuff," Darla says, leaning in. "Tanner's hot. I'm not gonna lie. A lot of us single ladies in town have had our eye on him for a long time. He is sexy with a capital X."

We laugh, and Darla looks around at us.

"What? He is!"

"Sexy starts with an S, drunk girl," I inform her. "But yes, you're right. He's hot and has excellent equipment, and believe me when I say that he knows what to do with it. And he just has this sweet way that he holds my face" —I reach for June to demonstrate—"like I'm the best treasure he has in the whole world, and he's all sweet and gentle and stuff."

"Yeah, yeah, with the sweet and gentle," June says, waving me off. "Go back to hot."

I grin, and when I realize that my glass is empty, I fill it back up. "Why do I have to tell all my secrets? Wolfe's sexy. Let's hear about his secret sexy ways. Luna?"

All of our attention turns to our hostess, who simply smiles.

"He's *bossy*. And it's the absolute best."

"Love it when Tanner gets bossy," I agree, and clink my glass to hers. "Does he do the pin-your-hands-above-your-head thing?"

"Sometimes," she says. "Mostly, it's just always really intense. I mean, he can be playful, too, but it's just *so* intense, and I think I might blow up from the heat, and then I don't blow up."

"We are *so* fucking drunk," Cordelia says with a snort. "And I haven't had sex in far too long."

"I highly recommend it," I inform her. "Frequently and as much as you can. I guess those two things mean the same thing."

"We're gonna need rides home," Darla decides. "These drinks were *strong*."

"I'm sure the guys could drive us," Luna says, but I shake my head.

"I think they were all going down to Lighthouse Pizza for beer." I narrow my eyes and reach for my phone. "But I could call Tanner and see."

"Actually, you can all crash here," Luna says. "I have four guest bedrooms and a couch, if you don't want to share."

"Who cares about sharing?" Mira fills her glass again. "Since we're staying, let's keep drinking."

"I really like your style," June says as she offers her glass for a refill.

SEPTEMBER 3, 2005

DEAR DIARY,

The eagle has landed. I repeat, the eagle has landed. Ha! This girl isn't a virgin anymore. Tanner's a gentleman, and I know he would have waited longer, but I just didn't want to. I love him, and he's so hot! How could a girl say no?

I couldn't.

Tanner rented us a hotel room down in Newport, and we had a romantic dinner from room service. Then, we took a walk on the beach before we went up to the room and made love.

Gosh, I love him so much!! He's my soulmate. My lobster. The peanut butter to my jelly.

He's everything I ever wanted in a man. I just know we're going to be together forever.

TTYL,

Sarah

Chapter Eighteen

Tanner

"How are you feeling, pretty girl?"

Sarah arrived home a little while ago, looking pretty rough after last night's shenanigans with her friends, but she wanted to take a walk on the beach to clear her head.

So, we are.

She tucks her hair behind her ear and sighs.

"I'm never drinking again."

I grin and kiss the top of her head as we stop just out of the surf's reach to watch the waves.

"Famous last words."

"No, really," she insists. "Never. We had so much fun, but I'm too old for that kind of drinking."

"Jesus, how many did you have?"

"More than I've had in the last ten years combined." I let out a low whistle, and she chuckles. "It was fun, though. The fresh air is helping my headache."

"I'll make you pancakes when we get back to the

house," I promise her, as we continue walking down the beach. "That'll help, too."

"That might be the only thing that sounds delicious. I will say that I'm very proud of myself for not throwing up."

"Did the others throw up?"

"I heard someone heaving in the bathroom. Not sure who it was." She winces at the thought. "Poor girl. But it's nice to have friends. Women who I can confide in and have fun with. We even talked about sex, and I don't remember the last time I did that."

"What about sex?" I slide my hand into hers and link our fingers.

"Well, *you* and sex, mostly."

I stare down at her. "What about *me*?"

"I can't tell you. It's girl talk. That's sacred. But don't worry, we talked about Wolfe, too. And toys. It was a long conversation."

"I see." I clear my throat, not sure how I feel about the idea of Sarah telling her friends about our sex life. "I lost a hundred bucks to Wolfe last night while playing pool. I think he cheats."

"How do you cheat at pool?" she wants to know.

"I don't know, but he has to be cheating. I told him I want a rematch so I can win my money back."

"Or, you could lose more."

"Your faith in me is astounding, my love."

She giggles, and then something on the sand catches her eye, so she bends over to pick it up.

"A baby sand dollar," she says in excitement. "It's

dead, but it's so small. And intact. I think I'll take it home."

She slips it into her pocket.

"Did you know that dead sand dollars, like that one, are said to be coins lost by mermaids?"

"I didn't know that." I smile down at her, enjoying the hell out of this. "Where did you hear that?"

"I read it somewhere when I was a kid. I've always loved the beach, and liked to learn everything I could about it. Anyway, I thought that was a fun little piece of folklore."

"Do you believe in mermaids?"

She frowns up at me. "Doesn't everyone? Mermaids, sirens, giant sea monsters. I think there's some truth to all of it."

"Hmm."

We're probably a mile down the beach from my house, so we turn to go back.

"We have that meeting with Belle tomorrow," I remind Sarah. "In the morning."

"I'm ready," she says. "Although, it's been pretty quiet lately. I'm starting to feel safe again."

"I don't want to drop our guard until we have confirmation that there's nothing to worry about."

"I know you're right. I just think it was all a series of unfortunate events that weren't even related to each other. Sometimes, life just sucks for a little while, and then it all evens out again." She shrugs a shoulder. "I think we're on the other side now."

I hope she's right. I *want* her to be right. But I won't relax until I know for sure that any risk has passed.

"I have something for you," she says with a bright smile as we get closer to the house. "I was going to save it for your birthday, but I don't think I can wait for July. That's forever away."

"It's May now," I remind her. "My birthday is in about six weeks."

"Forever away," she repeats. "I don't want to wait. I'll get you something else later."

"You don't have to get me anything at all, ever." I lean in and kiss her temple. "I have *you,* and that's plenty."

"You always say the nicest things."

"It's true."

"Well, whether it's true or not, I still have something for you."

We climb the steps up to the house, and once inside, Sarah turns to me, her eyes bright.

"I have to run out to the guesthouse. I'll be right back."

I narrow my eyes.

"I should go with you."

"Oh, please. It's fine. I'll be right back."

She hurries off, and I walk into the kitchen to start breakfast. I've just pulled everything out for pancakes when I hear the front door open and close, but when Sarah walks into the kitchen, she doesn't have anything in her hands.

"I want you to sit on the couch and close your eyes."

I tilt my head to the side, watching her. I would object, but she bites her lip in that way she does when she's excited, and I know that I can't tell her no.

So, I do as she asks. I sit on the couch and close my eyes, and I can hear her bustling about, rustling here and there.

Finally, she takes my hand.

"Don't open your eyes; just stand up."

She leads me to what feels like the center of the room, facing away from the beach, and then says, "Okay. Open them."

And when I do, my heart skips a beat.

Sitting on an easel is a watercolor painting. With blues and grays, it's an overcast day on the beach, with crashing waves. It's moody and thought provoking.

Absolutely beautiful.

But what steals the breath from my lungs is the couple on the sand, dancing.

"Sarah."

"I hope you like it," she whispers. "That moment on the beach when we danced was really special to me, and I wanted to capture it for you."

I step closer and examine the brush strokes, the love that she poured into the piece, and then I turn back to her and scoop her up into my arms, carrying her to the bedroom.

"Does this mean that you like it?"

"I don't have words," I admit as I set her on her feet and strip us both bare, and when we're finally in the bed,

I take both of her hands in one of my own and pin them over her head on the mattress.

A smile tickles her lips.

"What's so funny?"

"We talked about this last night."

I narrow my eyes. "About what?"

"The whole hands-pinned-over-the-head thing." She bites that lip again, and I lean down to brush my tongue over it. "It's hot, in case you didn't know."

"Why do you think I do it?"

She lets out a laugh, but when I nibble along her collarbone, she sighs and squirms under me. I can't stop kissing her, can't stop exploring every inch of her shoulders and chest, and when I dip lower, I have to let go of her hands.

Her fingers dive into my hair and hold on tightly as I move over her.

"I need you," I whisper against her ear as I move between her legs and slowly, inch by inch, sink inside of her.

"Oh, hell yes," she moans. "Oh, God, it's so fucking good."

"Every time." I brush a strand of hair off of her soft cheek. "Thank you for that incredible gift, Sarah."

"I'm so happy you like it."

I pull my hips back and then push back in again, making her gasp.

"You *really* like it."

"I really do." I kiss her, soft and slow, as I make love to

her, and when we both reach our climax, I hold her close, reveling in her as the shudders move through us both.

"I love you," I whisper.

"Same." Her mouth spreads in a satisfied smile. "Definitely same."

BELLE LOVEJOY IS the youngest sister to Amaryllis and Indigo, and she's been a private investigator for five years, after spending four in the military police with the Navy.

She's one badass woman.

"It's good to see you, Tanner," Belle says after shaking my hand and turns to Sarah. "And you probably don't remember me."

"I remember you," Sarah says. "You were just a kid when I left town. I'm closer in age to your older siblings."

"I always loved seeing you at Gordy's when you worked there as a teenager," Belle admits with a smile, and brushes her long dark hair over her shoulder. "I thought you were the prettiest girl in town."

Sarah's cheeks flush. "Well, thanks."

"But that's not why you're here," Belle continues. "Tell me what's been going on."

And so, we start from the beginning and tell her everything, from the break-in to the flat tire and everything in between.

"I think it's a lot of coincidence," Sarah says when I finish. "Bad luck."

"Maybe," Belle says, looking up from her notes. "I

don't like that someone left a note. If not for that, I'd be more inclined to agree with you."

"Perhaps they were just trying to scare me," Sarah continues, but Belle just blinks at her, and she sighs. "Or not."

"I think we should do more digging. I love our cops here in Huckleberry Bay, and get along well with all of them, but sometimes they can't devote the amount of time needed in cases like these. I'd like to start right away, making calls and such. If you'd like to hire me, that is."

"We would," I reply immediately. "I think we're both ready for some answers here. It's been several weeks, and Sarah just can't keep living her life constantly looking over her shoulder."

"I really would like to relax," Sarah admits. "I'd also like to be alone once in a while, just because I can."

"No one wants to feel like they have to have a chaperone all the time," Belle agrees. "Sarah, do you have any self-defense training or a concealed carry permit?"

"No and no," Sarah replies.

"Well then, I think that it's wise that you stick close to someone else until we get some answers. There is safety in numbers, you know?"

"Yep, I know." Sarah deflates. "What do we do now?"

"I'll start digging around online, make some calls, and do some research. Then, if I have to, I go out and investigate. I'll keep you posted whenever I find anything useful."

"Awesome." Sarah grins at Belle and claps her hands. "I feel like we're finally *doing* something."

"We are," I agree. "Thanks, Belle."

"My pleasure. Really. I love a puzzle, and we're going to put this one together. Don't worry, we'll figure it out."

When we're back on the sidewalk, headed toward the gallery where the car is parked, Sarah does a little skip.

"That went *very* well," she says. "I have a really good feeling about it. Also, how pretty is Belle Lovejoy? She's absolutely gorgeous, with that long hair and blue eyes, and I swear her skin is made out of porcelain. I wonder what her skin care regime is. How did she get into that line of work?"

"She was a cop in the Navy," I reply, then laugh when Sarah's jaw drops, and she stares at me. "It's true."

"Holy shit, that's badass."

"That's what I thought, too."

"Wow, so the Lovejoys all did well. Amaryllis is a doctor, Indigo is a killer real estate agent, and Bluebelle kicks ass for a living."

"Just don't call her Bluebelle, or she'll kick *your* ass."

"I like their names," she says with a sigh. "I like *them*. Okay, what's next on the list of things?"

"Why don't we pop into The Grind and grab a coffee? Take a load off for a minute?"

"I am totally game for that."

It's mid-morning, so the coffee shop isn't too busy when we walk in. We place our order and find a table by the windows to sit and enjoy ourselves.

"I don't remember the last time I sat in a coffee shop," Sarah says as she takes a sip from her huge mug of mocha. "Drinking out of a real mug rather than paper and having my pastry warmed up on a real plate."

"We have to stop and smell the roses sometimes." I watch her as she glances around the room and smiles at someone to her left. "Who do you see?"

"Montana, from Huckleberry Delight. She's really nice, too."

I look back and nod at Montana, then turn back to Sarah.

"There aren't many here who aren't nice, you know."

"Yeah, it seems I was blessed to be born to the only assholes in town." The smile doesn't waver as she takes a bite of her cranberry muffin, and I can't help but laugh.

"There might be one or two others."

"Name them."

I narrow my eyes and think it over.

"See? You can't. Because, for the most part, the people in this town are good. And I like it that way. Hell, if it had been any different, Scott and I might not have survived it. So, I'm grateful that we had kind people surrounding us."

"You have a good point." I reach over and take her hand. "When is your next shift at Gordy's?"

"Not for a few days. Sunny's just using me to fill in now in case someone needs vacation or calls in sick. I told her I'd try to come in on a moment's notice if something like that happened. So, basically, I'm just helping out here and there now."

"And how does that feel?"

"Good and bittersweet," she replies. "I really like my

job there. That's why I haven't quit altogether. But it also feels good to make my own hours and do my own thing. I've painted five pieces this week already. I know I won't always produce that much so fast, but I'm excited."

"You should be excited. I'm proud of you. And you don't have to completely quit Gordy's. I'm sure they appreciate you working in the capacity you are, in case they're ever in a jam."

"Exactly," she says with a nod. "Also, I never ended up needing to press charges against Angela. She came in and gave the money to Gordy, then tried to grovel to get her job back, but he turned her down. She's not happy about it, but I heard she's moving back down to Newport, anyway."

"I'm glad that worked out as well as it could have," I reply as her phone pings with a text.

"Oh, it's June. She wants me to meet her at the chapel. She wants to show Luna and me something. She actually mentioned that to us the other night. She must have a break in her work day."

"Should we head out?" I ask.

"Let's finish our coffee, and then we can head out. If you'll take me back to your place, I'll grab my car from there."

"Sounds good."

———

Sarah's been gone for about twenty minutes, headed to the chapel, when Belle calls.

"Hey, Belle. You're fast."

"Listen, I found something. Tell me Sarah's with you."

"Actually, she's not."

"Fuck. She's in trouble, Tanner."

Chapter Nineteen

Sarah

I park at the curb in front of the chapel and discover that I must have beat Luna, since mine is the only car here.

I hope it's a secret room, or maybe even a vault, or a secret burial place in the basement that June wants to show us. Sure, that's all dramatic and something out of a movie, but it could happen.

I stop to admire the hydrangeas that are starting to bloom out front, on either side of the steps that lead to the heavy wooden doors. The flowers around this building have always been beautiful for as long as I can remember. The ladies of the church tended to them, and it showed.

It still does, as the perennials come back every year and brighten up the whole block in bold blue and pink, red and purple.

With one last sniff of a bloom, I climb the stairs and turn the knob, finding it unlocked, and then I walk inside.

It's chilly in the chapel, so I tug my sweater around me a little tighter.

"June?" I move toward the two lone pews near the front of the sanctuary where the altar once lived. "June, I'm here!"

Huh, where is she? Maybe the basement?

I walk toward the door that leads downstairs, but before I can reach for the doorknob, something hits me from behind, and I feel myself falling.

And then I feel nothing at all.

My head is screaming. I try to reach up to touch the back of my head, but my hands are tied.

I open my eyes and find that I'm sitting in a chair, in the middle of the mostly empty chapel, and my hands are tied, palms up, to the arms of the chair.

"June?"

"Don't be silly."

My head whips around in time to see a woman, a *very* pregnant woman, walk across the room toward me.

"You're awake."

"*You?*" I shake my head in disbelief. "From the campground."

"I fucking *hate* to camp," she says, and then jerks a shoulder. "But, we do what we have to do, I guess. I'm Bridget, by the way. We never exchanged names."

"I don't know you, Bridget."

"No, you don't. But I know *you.*" Her eyes go cold,

and her lip turns up in a snarl. "You've ruined my entire fucking life."

"*Me*?" I shake my head again. "I don't see how that's possible, since I don't know you. Are you the one who broke into my house?"

"If you'd just *been* there, we wouldn't have gotten this far," she says impatiently. "Everything could have been resolved so quickly, but no, you just had to make it difficult at every turn. So really, we're here because of you."

"I see." Except, I don't see at all, and my heart is racing, pumping blood so loudly in my ears, I can hardly concentrate on what she's saying. "How did I hurt you, Bridget?"

Keep her talking. I just have to keep her talking.

I wish I could reach my phone so I could alert Tanner. He won't be expecting me home for a long time, so he'd have to reason to come find me.

My God, *no one* knows what's happening right now.

Don't panic, Sarah.

"I tried," she begins and waddles around the chapel, rubbing her hands over her huge belly. "I really, *really* tried to be everything that he needed me to be. I still try. I'm submissive, I follow orders, I'm demure and kind, and I fuck him whenever he wants me to. I've done *everything*, but no matter what I try, it's never enough."

She turns to me now and bares her teeth in frustration.

"Because I'm not *you*."

"What?" But it all starts to click into place. "Wait, are you Anthony's new wife?"

"He's *mine*," she shrieks. "But he throws you in my face constantly. *If you were more like Sarah, I'd love you more. Do it like Sarah. Talk like Sarah. Sarah, Sarah, Sarah.* For fuck's sake, I'm sick of hearing about you."

There's a thump behind us, and Bridget's head whips around, and right before my very eyes, her demeanor completely changes.

She shrinks in on herself, casts her eyes to the floor, and seems to...wither.

"You haven't finished." He tsks and walks around the chair so I can see him.

He hasn't changed in the months since I last saw him. Anthony was always handsome, with a full head of dark hair and a tall, lean body. And when he smiles, his teeth are white and straight.

But the smile doesn't reach his eyes, and I know that there's no good that lives in him.

"Well, hello, darling."

"I'm not your darling."

He shakes his head. "You disappoint me, Sarah."

"How is that possible? I left with literally nothing but my clothes. You got what you wanted, Anthony. A new young woman and no ties to me."

"You didn't beg."

It's said so simply, so effortlessly, that all I can do is blink at him.

"What?"

"You." He walks closer. "Didn't." Gets down in my face. "Beg."

"For what?"

"Me."

He backs up and walks away, circling the space.

"You didn't play the game, Sarah, and that really disappointed me. It really *hurt* me."

"Right." I roll my eyes, but my stomach is in knots. "I couldn't hurt you. You didn't give a shit about me."

"He loves you!" Bridget yells, and her bottom lip trembles as her eyes fill with tears. Her hands are fisted at her sides, and her chest heaves. "I've done everything I can to be you. I even dyed my hair blonde. He always tells me that if I could just be more like *you*, he'd love me."

I glance Anthony's way, but he says nothing. Just watches me.

Why did I ever think this creepy-ass jerk was hot?

"I've done everything," she says again. "Everything you asked me to. I broke into her house. I followed her to the campground. I even burned down her apartment."

I choke on my own spit as I gasp. "You burned down the garage?"

She nods.

"And you've been following me."

"Yes," she says immediately, nodding her head almost manically. "Yes, I've never been far away. I go through your things all the time. I had to get good at disarming security, but I'm a pro at it now."

"The flat tire," I whisper. "No gas in my car. Even the ChapStick."

"All of those," she says, still nodding. "And more you haven't found yet. All for you."

She turns to Anthony again and hurries to him, throwing herself in his arms.

"Please love me. Please love *us*. I'm having your baby, and we just want you to love us."

"My God," I say, watching her eyes go mad as she stares up at Anthony. "He's driven you mad."

She whirls around, her face full of fury as she rushes over and slaps me across the face.

"I'm not CRAZY!"

"Bridget." His voice is firm, leaving no room for argument.

"Sorry," she says, and casts her eyes down again. "What do you want me to do to prove that you should love me?"

"You know what you have to do. What I've wanted you to do for months. You've been too afraid, wasted time. The campground was the ideal place. It would have been so easy to push her off a cliff, but you failed."

Bridget turns her eyes to mine, and they fill with tears again. I can see a war raging inside of her, and for the first time, I almost feel sorry for her.

"You want her to *kill* me."

"Well, of course."

"Because I didn't play the game of begging you not to divorce me."

"No one *leaves* me, Sarah. We had a contract, in the eyes of the law. You're not allowed to just walk out."

"You kicked me out because you'd found *her* and wanted to marry her."

"That's so sweet," Bridget whispers.

"Yes, well, you didn't try very hard to fight it, did you?" he asks me, ignoring his pregnant wife.

"When I told you I'd contest the prenup, you punched me in the face."

"I don't give a fuck about the goddamn prenup!" His face is purple as he yells now, just as wild as Bridget. They're both absolutely nuts. "You were supposed to want *me*!"

"Well, I don't. I gave you what you wanted, and I left so you could make a life with her."

I nod toward the woman who's weeping now.

"You have what you wanted. A much younger woman who wants to give you a family."

He's shaking with anger, his body vibrating with the fury rolling through him.

And I know that unless a miracle happens, I'm not going to make it out of here alive. I want to panic. I want to beg and cry and scream.

God, I want to see Tanner, to tell him how much I love him.

"You know what you have to do to make me love you," Anthony says to Bridget and takes a deep breath, calming himself down. "Make it look like an accident. Or like she did it herself."

Tears continue to run down Bridget's face as she pulls a butcher knife out of her bag and walks to me.

I'm sorry, she mouths.

"Don't do this." I'm not begging. I'm not whining. It's a calm statement, but Bridget just shakes her head and holds my hand down while the blade hovers over my wrist. "He won't love you, even if you do this. You'll be charged with murder, and he'll go free. You're just doing his dirty work, Bridget."

"No," she says and sniffs. "It's the only way."

The blade touches my skin but doesn't pierce it, which is a miracle, because her hand is shaking violently.

"For fuck's sake," Anthony says as he stomps over and wraps his hand around Bridget's wrist, and pushes.

The pain is swift and sharp as the blade slices into my wrist, through the tender flesh and into tendons and ligaments...and veins.

When the blade swipes out, the blood starts. I swallow hard and strain against the restraints.

"Oh, God," Bridget murmurs. "I hate the sight of blood."

"You'll finish it, or I'll do the same to you and that brat growing inside of you."

Bridget's eyes flash and then fill with hurt as she turns to me.

"Told you," I whisper, feeling queasy. I'm not a fan of blood either, and it's running in a small river down my hand.

"DO IT!" Anthony screams, and Bridget jumps, then walks to my other side.

Just when I think I'm about to pass out, people pour into the room from both the front and the rear entrances.

"Freeze!" I think that's Callum's voice. "Drop the weapon, and put your hands on your heads!"

"Baby." Tanner's suddenly at my side, his hands all

over me. "Where are you hurt? What—oh, God. She's cut! We need an ambulance."

"Wrist," I whisper, feeling funny.

"You're okay," he assures me and pushes something over the wound. It hurts, but I know it'll stop the bleeding.

I look over to see Anthony on his stomach on the ground, glaring up at me. Bridget is sitting on a pew, her hands tied behind her back, and she continues to cry.

"Feel bad for her," I say, as Tanner wraps me in his arms. "He's ruined her life."

"Yeah, well, she almost killed you, so I'm just going to be angry for a while." He kisses my face, my lips, as someone unties me from the chair.

"How bad?"

"Scott?"

"Right here," he says and tosses the ropes aside. "How bad is it?"

"One wrist slashed," Tanner says briskly. "And she's in shock. Probably from the whole incident more than the cut."

"Cut kinda hurts," I remind him.

"Sarah!"

June and Luna are here but are asked to go outside by the cops while they secure the scene.

"Want out of here."

"Okay, baby." Tanner kisses my forehead, and I notice for the first time that his hands are shaking.

"You okay?" I ask him.

"No. No, I'm not okay. But I will be."

"How did you know?"

"She okay?" I glance up at the voice and see Belle standing next to us.

"You found something."

She grins at me and nods. "Yeah, I did. And it's a good thing because it looks like this party was about to go south real fast."

"What did you find?"

"Baby, we can talk about this later."

"I want to know."

Belle squats in front of me and licks her lips. "Bridget's parents reported her as a missing person a couple of months ago. There's been no trace of her until last week when she used her debit card to rent a camper."

I feel my eyes go wide. "How did they miss that?"

"Yeah, someone dropped the ball. I found she used her card a couple of times after that, once here in Huckleberry Bay. Knowing her connection to your ex, the puzzle fit together."

"Belle called me and asked if you were with me, and when I said no, we raced over here," Tanner finishes. "And her hunch was right."

"Thank God."

Scott arrives with a gurney. "We're taking you to the hospital. You're going to need stitches for that, and I want your head checked for concussion."

"I'm not arguing."

The guys help me up onto the gurney, but before they wheel me out, I stop them.

"Take me to her."

"Sarah," Scott begins, but I stop him.

"Take me to her."

He wheels me over, and Bridget looks up at me. She looks pitiful and sad. And lost.

"There's help, you know. He really messed with your head, but it doesn't always have to be like that. You and your baby can get help and be safe."

She swallows hard and nods. "Yeah, well, I'm probably going to jail, anyway."

"Maybe. But you can turn this around. Just stay far away from me."

She nods again. "I won't be back."

"Do you want to talk to the asshole motherfucker?" Scott asks.

"Absolutely not."

"IT'S GOOD TO BE HOME." I cuddle Petunia close and kiss her soft cheek. As soon as I walked through the door, she came racing to meet me. "I was only gone one night, but you'd think it was a year, as far as she's concerned."

"She knew something wasn't right," Tanner replies and scratches the cat behind her ears. "What do you say to a walk on the beach? Are you up for it?"

"It's a cut on my arm, Tanner, not a stab to the heart. I don't even have a concussion. Let's do it."

It's a sunny spring day, and the wind is surprisingly light when we get down to the sand and kick off our shoes. Hand in hand, we set off toward the water to walk by the shoreline.

"It's wild how much can happen in the span of twenty-four hours." I blow out a breath and then take in a deep one, filling my lungs with the salty air that always seems to revitalize me. "I'm really, *really* glad it's over, Tanner."

"Me, too." He hugs me to him, cradling me against his chest, and kisses the top of my hair. He didn't leave me at the hospital for a minute. He even slept in the chair next to the bed and was glued to my side until they released me this morning. "I was scared out of my mind when we rushed into that chapel."

"I'm surprised the police let you in," I admit. "They don't usually do that on cop shows."

"I didn't really give them a choice. And I needed to get to you."

I look up at him and see the worry, the love, in his eyes.

"I'm okay. I really am. I'm pressing charges, and June's pressing charges, and I don't think either of them will be bothering me again. Oh, Wolfe and Zeke are also pressing arson charges."

Suddenly, Tanner takes my hand, wraps his other arm around my back, and begins to lead me in a slow dance here on the sand, with the water singing around us.

"I was so worried that I wouldn't get to do this again," he says with a tender smile. "That I wouldn't get to do a lot of things with you."

"You're not getting rid of me that easy."

"I don't ever want to get rid of you. In fact..."

He stops swaying and then *kneels*.

Tanner pulls a ring out of his pocket and holds it up to me.

"I've waited a *very* long time to do this. I think we both had to live through a whole different life to circle back around to each other, and I'm glad we did. It gave us both insight into what really matters and what we want out of life.

"For me, that's you. I want to be by your side for the rest of my days, rooting for you, building each other up. I want to plant our own roots here in Huckleberry Bay with a family. I want a life with you, Sarah. I know, in my heart, that no matter how long I have with you, it'll never be enough, but I want every single minute of it. I'm greedy like that."

I don't even bother to brush away the happy tears falling down my cheeks.

"Will you marry me, pretty girl?"

I laugh and nod, and then he slips the gorgeous diamond onto my finger and stands to hug me close.

"Of course, I'll marry you."

He kisses me, slow and easy, tickling my lips with his. And when he pulls back, he cups my cheeks in his hands.

"I love you so much, I ache with it, Sarah."

"I love you, too." I tip my forehead to his and hold on tight. "Now, let's go get started on those roots."

He grins and kisses me softly, then more urgently.

"As you wish."

JUNE 20, 2022

DEAR DIARY,

It's been one hell of a crazy month. I just got word that Anthony and Bridget have both been sentenced to prison. They plead guilty to all charges, which actually shocked me, but I suspect that Anthony's attorney talked him into it. They won't get out of jail for a long, long time. I feel bad because Bridget gave birth in prison, and her family will raise the baby. But it's probably for the best.

It seems like every day I find something new that Bridget messed with. Nothing has been dangerous, just odd. And, if I hadn't known that it was her, I would have felt like I was losing my mind when I found it.

I think that's what she wanted because Anthony was making her lose her's.

But, life is moving forward, and it's never been better! I moved in with Tanner, and we converted the guesthouse into a studio for me. I'm working hard to succeed as an artist. It's scary and exciting, all at the same time! There are some fun projects ahead that I can't wait to dive into, including work for Three Sisters and a birthday project that a sweet older man has hired me to do for his wife.

What a wonderful life I have. I'm so grateful!

TTYL,

Sarah

Epilogue

June

Three Months Later

God, why does he have to be so...*Apollo*? So tall and dark and muscled. So fucking *hot* that it makes me grouchy.

He's standing over there with Wolfe and Zeke, having a beer and joking around. We're all at Lighthouse Pizza, celebrating the reopening of Wolfe's workshop, now that the building has been rebuilt, and they can start taking customers again.

I'm happy for them. It's been a rough time with the investigation and then rebuilding.

And now we know who burned it to the ground.

I glance over and see Sarah laughing with Tanner as he tries to show her how to play pool.

My God, we almost lost her.

A shiver runs through me at the thought, and I turn to grab my own beer, taking a pull.

"What are you doing over here all by yourself?"

I turn and find that Apollo's walked over to join me.

The man drives me up the goddamn wall, in the best and worst ways.

"Just taking it all in."

"You did a good job on the garage, June."

"I just pulled the crew together." I shrug a shoulder. "You know I've been busy with the inn. I didn't have much extra time to be at the garage."

"Well, the crew worked their magic. It's way better than it was before it burned."

"It should be. That was a fifty-year-old building. This one is brand new and state of the art. Why are you over here, bugging me?"

He grins, and it makes my girl parts turn to goo.

Damn him.

"Maybe I just like the look of you."

"Right." I snort and take another sip of beer. "I'm not really your type, Apollo."

"Oh, I think you know you're wrong about that." He moves in closer, and that's all it takes for my heart to beat in overtime. "I'm not the only one that feels the chemistry here. It's why we're always swiping at each other."

"So what of it?" I sip my beer and will the butterflies in my stomach to calm the hell down. "Maybe I like swiping at you."

"I think that just once, we should give into this

magnetic pull that seems to be here, and get it out of our systems. Then you can go back to hating me."

I narrow my eyes on him and stare at his lips.

He grins again.

Damn him.

"This changes absolutely *nothing*."

He nods, takes my beer out of my hand, and sets it aside. "Agreed."

"We tell no one."

"Also agreed."

"And it happens exactly *once*."

"Now, that, I can't guarantee." He rocks back on his heels. "Let's call it one *night*."

I feel my eyebrows climb in surprise. "Oh, it's like that, is it?"

"Yeah, it's like that. You in or not?"

Against my better judgment, I grab my purse. "I'm in. Damn it."

ARE you ready for June and Apollo's story? You can get all of the information for Chapel Bend here:

https://www.kristenprobyauthor.com/chapel-bend

About the Author

Kristen Proby has published more than sixty titles, many of which have hit the USA Today, New York Times and Wall Street Journal Bestsellers lists.

Kristen and her husband, John, make their home in her hometown of Whitefish, Montana with their two cats and dog.

facebook.com/booksbykristenproby

instagram.com/kristenproby

bookbub.com/profile/kristen-proby

goodreads.com/kristenproby

Newsletter Sign Up

I hope you enjoyed reading this story as much as I enjoyed writing it! For upcoming book news, be sure to join my newsletter! I promise I will only send you news-filled mail, and none of the spam. You can sign up here:

https://mailchi.mp/kristenproby.com/newsletter-sign-up

Also by Kristen Proby:

Other Books by Kristen Proby

The Single in Seattle Series
The Secret
The Surprise
The Scandal

The With Me In Seattle Series

Come Away With Me
Under The Mistletoe With Me
Fight With Me
Play With Me
Rock With Me
Safe With Me
Tied With Me

Breathe With Me
Forever With Me
Stay With Me
Indulge With Me
Love With Me
Dance With Me
Dream With Me
You Belong With Me
Imagine With Me
Shine With Me
Escape With Me
Flirt With Me
Change With Me
Take a Chance With Me

Check out the full series here: https://www.
kristenprobyauthor.com/with-me-in-seattle

The Big Sky Universe

Love Under the Big Sky
Loving Cara
Seducing Lauren
Falling for Jillian
Saving Grace

The Big Sky
Charming Hannah

Kissing Jenna
Waiting for Willa
Soaring With Fallon

Big Sky Royal
Enchanting Sebastian
Enticing Liam
Taunting Callum

Heroes of Big Sky
Honor
Courage
Shelter

Check out the full Big Sky universe here:
https://www.kristenprobyauthor.com/under-the-big-sky

Bayou Magic
Shadows
Spells
Serendipity

Check out the full series here: https://www.
kristenprobyauthor.com/bayou-magic

The Romancing Manhattan Series

All the Way

Also by Kristen Proby:

All it Takes
After All

Check out the full series here: https://www.
kristenprobyauthor.com/romancing-manhattan

The Boudreaux Series

Easy Love
Easy Charm
Easy Melody
Easy Kisses
Easy Magic
Easy Fortune
Easy Nights

Check out the full series here: https://www.
kristenprobyauthor.com/boudreaux

The Fusion Series

Listen to Me
Close to You
Blush for Me
The Beauty of Us
Savor You

Check out the full series here: https://www.
kristenprobyauthor.com/fusion

From 1001 Dark Nights

Easy With You
Easy For Keeps
No Reservations
Tempting Brooke
Wonder With Me
Shine With Me

Kristen Proby's Crossover Collection

Soaring with Fallon, A Big Sky Novel

Wicked Force: A Wicked Horse Vegas/Big Sky Novella
By Sawyer Bennett

All Stars Fall: A Seaside Pictures/Big Sky Novella
By Rachel Van Dyken

Hold On: A Play On/Big Sky Novella
By Samantha Young

Worth Fighting For: A Warrior Fight Club/Big Sky
Novella
By Laura Kaye

Crazy Imperfect Love: A Dirty Dicks/Big Sky Novella
By K.L. Grayson

Nothing Without You: A Forever Yours/Big Sky Novella
By Monica Murphy

**Check out the entire Crossover Collection
here:** https://www.kristenprobyauthor.com/kristen-
proby-crossover-collection

Made in the USA
Columbia, SC
16 August 2024

40532672R00183